All he wanted was to take his girls for a ride and picnic.

His girls. When had he begun thinking of Erin and her daughter that way?

One look at Erin when she stepped outside and he was a goner. "You look great."

"Thanks, cowboy." Grinning, she eyed him up and down. "You don't look so bad yourself." She called for her daughter. "Mr. Ritter's here, honey. Let's go."

"Would you have a problem if she just called me Kent?"

"I guess not. But I've taught her to respect her elders."

"Elders?" Kent winced. "Maybe I should have brought my cane."

Erin's laughter sparkled like summer sunshine.

She explained to her daughter that since Kent was now a good friend, she could use his first name.

The little girl grinned. "Does that mean that you'll be calling him 'honey' and 'sweetie' like my friend's mom does her dad?"

Kent stifled a gasp as he slid a glance at Erin. They were names he'd never expected a woman to call him. So why didn't they suddenly seem so bad?

Award-winning author **Myra Johnson** writes emotionally gripping stories about love, life and faith. She is a two-time finalist for the ACFW Carol Award and winner of the 2005 RWA Golden Heart® Award. Married since 1972, Myra and her husband have two married daughters and seven grandchildren. Although Myra is a native Texan, she and her husband now reside in North Carolina, sharing their home with two pampered rescue dogs.

Books by Myra Johnson

Love Inspired

Rancher for the Holidays
Her Hill Country Cowboy
Hill Country Reunion
The Rancher's Redemption

Visit the Author Profile page at Harlequin.com.

The Rancher's Redemption

Myra Johnson

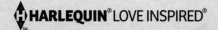

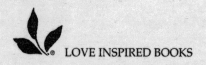

LOVE INSPIRED BOOKS

Recycling programs for this product may not exist in your area.

ISBN-13: 978-1-335-47917-4

The Rancher's Redemption

Copyright © 2019 by Myra Johnson

www.Harlequin.com

Printed in U.S.A.

When thou passest through the waters,
I will be with thee; and through the rivers,
they shall not overflow thee: when thou walkest
through the fire, thou shalt not be burned;
neither shall the flame kindle upon thee.
—*Isaiah* 43:2

For my brother Ralph, who settled in the Texas Hill Country more than sixty years ago to pursue his ranching dreams. This city-girl author will always treasure childhood memories of horseback rides and other Hill Country adventures during our fun family visits.

Chapter One

A sunny azure sky overhead, contented cattle grazing beside a tree-shaded pond, field upon field of bluebonnets stretching toward the horizon—in all his thirty-six years, Kent Ritter had yet to see anything prettier than an April day in the Texas Hill Country.

Until he rode out to round up a couple of strays and came upon a waiflike stranger sitting cross-legged beneath an oak tree.

His oak tree. On *his* land.

Facing the opposite direction, the girl didn't seem aware of Kent's approach. An assortment of grasses and twigs lay beside her on a multicolored quilt. She bent low over something in her lap, chin-length auburn curls falling toward her face and her fingers flying.

Not of a mind to announce his presence until he had a better idea of what she was up to, Kent pulled on his cutting horse's reins with a whispered "Whoa, Jasmine."

He guessed he wasn't as quiet as he'd thought, because his visitor's head shot up and she turned with a startled gasp. As she scrambled to her feet, whatever she'd been working on fell to the quilt. Panic filled her eyes, but her stance—fists clenched at her sides, feet apart as if preparing for combat—sent a different message: *don't mess with me!*

Kent's stomach fell straight to his boot heels. Clearly, this fully grown *woman* wasn't the truant teenager he'd assumed her to be. The fine lines at the corners of her eyes suggested late twenties or early thirties—much closer to Kent's age than he suddenly felt comfortable with, since his initial curious concern now vied with an undeniable and completely inappropriate attraction. Yep, more than likely, this woman's appearance had something to do with the unsettling letter he'd received two days ago, the one he'd been doing his dead level best to ignore.

He clenched his jaw. "If you're from the Juniper Bluff Historical Society, you can leave right now. This is *still* private property."

"I'm so sorry." Looking both startled and confused, the woman dropped to her knees and began gathering her things into the center of the quilt. "I was just out exploring, and I don't know anything about the historical society. I'm actually new in town and—" Her hands shook so hard that she kept dropping everything.

First he'd jumped to conclusions, and now he'd scared the poor lady half to death. "Hey, it's okay." Afraid she'd have a heart attack, Kent dismounted and strode over to help. "Ma'am, it's okay, really."

As he drew closer, he saw what she'd been making—a basket woven from twigs and dry pasture grass. He picked it up and studied the intricate design. Blades of grass had been twisted and shaped to resemble miniature bluebonnets and woven into the outside of the basket. Between two of the flowers, a thinner, more pliable twig formed the letter *A*.

Glancing up, Kent found the woman standing at the edge of the quilt, arms crossed and her expression wary. He held the basket out to her. "You made this? Just now?"

"Well, yes. But not just now, exactly." Taking the basket, she offered a guilty frown. "I—I've been here most of the day."

Even if she wasn't a historical society snoop, Kent ought to feel a lot more annoyed that a perfect stranger had been trespassing on his property—he'd chased off ignorant city kids looking to go cow tipping on a dare, hunters who'd unknowingly crossed boundaries, even a few lost hikers and trail riders. But never in all the years he'd been ranching had he come upon anyone quite like this nervous and oh-so-pretty artisan.

She tugged on the quilt, drawing attention to the fact that he was standing on the edge. Stepping off into the grass, he bent and grabbed the two corners closest to him. When all her craft supplies—bits and pieces of *his* pasture—were folded inside the quilt, she hugged the bundle against her chest. Her chin rose in defiance. "You really ought to put up signs. How was I supposed to know this was someone's property?"

Kent's jaw dropped. "Miles of barbed wire fencing wasn't enough of a clue? How'd you even end up this far from the main road?"

Glancing around, the woman started looking panicky again. "Um, which way *is* the road?"

Okay, this was just too much—probably a good thing because, at the moment, Kent's annoyance was a whole lot easier to deal with than being discombobulated by a damsel in distress. He whipped his tan felt Resistol from his head and slapped it against his thigh. "You ride?"

"Ride?"

"Yeah, ride. Because the easiest and fastest way for me to get you back to the road is if I take you on my horse."

She eyed the big black mare uneasily. "Thanks, but I'd rather walk."

"You realize we're a couple miles in, right?"

"That far?" A swallow tracked up and down her throat, so thin and delicate and lovely it made Kent's chest ache. "I must have explored farther than I thought."

"Guess so." He inched his gaze upward, only to find himself riveted by a pair of eyes bluer than a whole field of bluebonnets. With a rough cough, he slammed his hat back onto his head. "So. You want a ride to the road or not?"

After an uneasy glance in all directions, she peeked at her watch. "Oh, no, is it really nearly three?"

"Afraid so. That a problem?"

"Yes, it's a problem." She was already striding toward Jasmine. "My daughter gets out of school in twenty minutes, and I'm going to be late."

Daughter. Which meant there had to be a dad in the picture. Wildly, that came as both a disappointment and a huge relief. Kent caught up with her at the mare's side, and then *he* was the nervous one. Riding double—what had he been thinking? Sure, he could let her ride while he led Jasmine from the ground. After his three tours of duty as a navy corpsman in Afghanistan, hiking a couple of miles over rough pastureland was a walk in the park.

Just one problem, though. This *walk in the park*—the

most direct route back to the road—covered a section of his property where he'd recently spotted a rattler's den. The lady was plumb lucky she hadn't encountered one while traipsing across the pastures with bare ankles and wearing those flimsy sneakers, or instead of offering her a ride, he might have been administering first aid from the snakebite kit in his saddlebag—and only if he'd found her in time.

Taking hold of Jasmine's bridle, he brought the horse's head up from the clump of grass she'd been munching on. "So," he said, teeth clenched, "if we're gonna get up close and personal on the back of my horse, we should at least introduce ourselves. Name's Kent Ritter." He stuck out his right hand.

She stared at it for a moment, then released her hold on the quilt long enough to accept his handshake. "I'm Erin. Erin Dearborn."

Pretty girl, pretty name…

The sooner he got this woman back to the road and off his property the better.

When Erin decided to take a drive down a country road in search of interesting items for her basketry creations, doubling up on horseback with a perfect stranger was not how she saw her day unfolding. Served her right for her city-girl ignorance. Before parking her car along the roadside, she hadn't passed a house for miles. The barbed wire fence? Well, those were everywhere out this way. Why should she assume it meant keep out?

The cowboy climbed into the saddle first, then had Erin pass him her quilt bundle. He removed his left boot from the stirrup and shifted his leg forward. Pointing toward the empty stirrup, he instructed, "Put your foot here, grab my arm and swing your other leg over."

She did as she was told, and with a breathtaking burst of motion, she found herself straddling the horse's rump just behind the saddle. The man shoved the wadded-up quilt around behind him, and she hugged it close, grateful for the space the bundle created between her chest and the lean, muscular torso in front of her. "I could have walked, you know. I'm not a wimp."

"Uh-huh." The cowboy's laconic reply said he didn't quite believe her. "If you didn't get lost. Or snakebit."

Her eyebrows shot up. She sat a little straighter. "Snakes? There are snakes out here?"

"This is the Texas Hill Country. Of course there are snakes." He glanced over his shoulder with a snort. "Weather's warming up, rattlers are getting more active—"

"Rattlesnakes?" Skin crawling, Erin drew her knees higher on the horse's sides.

The man chuckled. "Rattlesnakes can't fly. Anyway, Jasmine's got a keen sense for snakes. She won't take us anywhere near one."

"That's… That's good to know." After a couple of calming breaths, Erin relaxed her legs.

Picking up the reins, the cowboy suggested Erin might want to hold on.

"To what?"

"To *me*." He reached behind and found her right wrist, drawing her arm around his waist. "I don't bite, I promise."

Erin didn't have a reply to that. But when the horse—Jasmine?—began to move, holding on felt like a really good idea. The horse's rhythmic, rocking gait reassured her, though, and before long, Erin was almost enjoying the ride—or would be, if not for the nearness of the man in front of her.

"So," he said, "do you make a habit of wandering across private property to do your—whatever that art stuff is called?"

"It's basketry. And no. I just thought—" She forced out a sharp sigh. What was the point of explaining? He'd just pile on more ridicule for her foolishness. And he'd be right. She had no business wasting her time on such a useless hobby when she should be getting serious about the interior design career she'd postponed so many years ago. Scary stuff, starting over after a divorce. Especially when starting over felt a lot more like starting from scratch.

"Basketry, huh?" the cowboy harrumphed. "Next time you're looking for twigs and stuff, maybe check with the property owner first."

"Duly noted."

When he deftly opened a pasture gate without dismounting, then guided the horse through and closed the gate behind them, Erin couldn't help being impressed.

Off to their right, a herd of black cattle grazed, their musky smells mingling with the earthy scents of grass and cedar. "Are those your cows?" Erin asked.

"Mmm-hmm. Minus the two still off somewhere by themselves because I got sidetracked rescuing you."

"Look, I'm sorry, Mr..." She'd already forgotten his name.

"Ritter," he supplied, sounding irritable. "And don't worry about it. Road's just up ahead. Tell me where you left your car."

They'd come a different way from the route Erin had taken cross-country, so nothing looked familiar.

Noticing a dilapidated two-story farmhouse off to the right, which she didn't remember passing on her drive out, she decided her car must be up the road to the left.

"I'm pretty sure it's that way," she said, pointing. Another glance at her watch made her stomach clench. School would be letting out about now, and it was only Avery's second day at Juniper Bluff Elementary. The almost seven-year-old had suffered enough trauma in her short life. She didn't need to wonder if Mommy had forgotten her. "Can you hurry, please? My daughter's going to be so worried."

"All right, hold on." After guiding the horse through another gate, the cowboy made sure Erin's hold was secure before clucking to the horse.

Unprepared for the burst of speed, Erin gasped and tightened her grip around Mr. Ritter's waist, the quilt bundle trapped against his back. They galloped past a weathered barn and onto a gravel lane that ran alongside the old farmhouse. Even as they sped by, Erin couldn't miss the peeling paint, sagging porches and flower beds overgrown with weeds. An unexpected pang of sadness struck—this must be where the grumpy cowboy lived.

He slowed the horse to make the left turn onto the road, then picked up speed again. Seconds later, peering around the cowboy, Erin glimpsed her dark blue Camry where she'd left it parked on the shoulder. By the time Mr. Ritter halted his horse next to her car, her heart was pounding as hard as if she'd run the two miles on foot.

He swung his right leg forward over the horse's neck and dropped to the ground, then reached up to help Erin dismount. The quilt still smashed against her chest, she backed toward her car door. "Well, um…thank you for the ride." *Deep breath*. She tugged her keys from her jeans pocket and nearly dropped them before she could press the unlock button on the key fob. "I'm sorry again about trespassing, and you don't have to worry about me ever bothering you again."

Without waiting for his response, she climbed into the car and shoved the quilt onto the passenger seat. She could only hope she hadn't crushed the special basket she'd been creating for Avery. After making sure the cowboy and his horse had moved out of the way, she executed an awkward U-turn. As she drove away, a glance in her rearview mirror showed the cowboy back in the saddle but watching from the same spot.

She shivered. *Okay, God, what was that all about?* Her first week in town and she had to run afoul of one of the residents. Not to mention having her life flash before her eyes on that wild ride. Horses were her older brother Greg's department, at least vicariously. His daughter rode for her college team, and as CFO for the family's San Antonio philanthropic organization, Greg had negotiated a partnership with a Juniper Bluff guest ranch to sponsor riding camps for disadvantaged kids.

But Erin, Greg and their middle sibling, Shaun, had grown up 100 percent city kids. Greg was now a successful businessman, and Shaun served as an ordained minister on the mission field. Their late father had been a highly respected San Antonio pediatrician, and their mother, also in heaven now, had founded her own interior design company. Erin had hoped to follow in her mother's footsteps, but those career plans had short-circuited not long after she'd met Payne Dearborn.

Fresh out of med school and interning at a Dallas hospital, Payne had been on duty when Erin's roommate at the University of North Texas tripped on the stairs at a shopping mall and broke her ankle. Erin had to drive her to the ER, where the handsome intern had asked for Erin's number. One date led to another and another, and within a year, they were engaged. Erin spent her last semester of college planning their June wedding, and afterward her whole world had revolved around Payne.

If only someone else had been in the ER that day. If only she hadn't given Payne her number, gone out with him the first time, fallen desperately in love with him—or, more accurately, with the idea of marrying a doctor just like her kind, caring, devoted dad. Because Payne Dearborn had turned out to be *nothing* like Erin's dad. Why hadn't she recognized the signs—if not before the wedding, then certainly before bringing a child into the marriage? As the years passed, Payne came to depend more and more on alcohol to relieve the stress of his profession. And the more he drank, the more his cruel side came out.

Nine years, a broken collarbone and entirely too many bruises later, Erin had had enough. Though Payne had never laid a hand on Avery, Erin could no longer take the chance. For both their sakes, she got out.

Brushing away an unexpected tear, she shoved the memories aside and concentrated on her driving. A few minutes later, she pulled into the nearly deserted school parking lot. As she glanced around for Avery, her heart plummeted. Surely, the little girl wouldn't have accepted a ride from someone else.

Then the fair-haired first-grade teacher Erin had met when she'd enrolled Avery on Monday strode from the building, her hand wrapped around Avery's. Spying her mom, Avery lit up with a huge grin. She broke free from the teacher and galloped toward the car faster than the grumpy cowboy's big black horse.

Erin reached across to shove the passenger door open, then stuffed the quilt bundle into the back seat. "Hi, honey! Sorry I'm late."

"It's okay, Mommy." The little girl swiped messy auburn curls out of her eyes as she bounded into the car. "While we waited for you, Miss Adams let me help her feed the gerbils."

"Wow, gerbils—how fun!" Erin looked past her daughter to cast an apologetic smile toward the teacher now leaning in the open door. "Thank you for looking after her. I totally lost track of time." *Among other things*.

"My pleasure. Avery was a big help." With a reassuring smile, the teacher added, "And she's doing fine. Already making friends. Aren't you, Avery?"

"I am, Mommy. My new bestest friend is Eva Austin. She's kind of new at school, too, 'cause she used to be homeschooled. She lives on a ranch and has her very own pony."

"A pony. How special." Erin returned Miss Adams's wave as the teacher closed Avery's door.

Apparently, just about everyone in this little Hill Country town had some connection with horses and ranching. She might have been born and raised a Texan, but her exposure to cowboy culture was pretty much limited to the TV Westerns she'd watched as a kid on the oldies channel.

What could Greg have been thinking? Her big brother had assured her that moving to Juniper Bluff could mean a fresh start, a chance to leave the past behind and figure out what she wanted to do with the rest of her life. But couldn't she have done so just as well in San Antonio, maybe rented a small apartment near Greg's place? If she really did have hopes of launching an interior design business, wouldn't her prospects be a lot stronger in the city? The part-time job Greg had arranged for her at a Juniper Bluff gift shop would never pay enough to support her and Avery for the long term.

And she *had* to take some positive action soon, while she still clung to what few remnants of self-esteem Payne Dearborn hadn't managed to crush.

Riding out to search again for those two stray heifers, Kent hoped getting back to work would distract him from dealing with his unexpected visitor. Because she'd sure enough distracted him. And while he appreciated a few diversions at the moment, that kind he could do without.

Recalling her reaction at the mention of the snakes, though, he allowed himself another brief chuckle. He also made a mental note to ask his neighbor LeRoy if he'd come by one day soon and help him deal with those rattlers—preferably without the use of a rifle. Kent loved ranching, but he despised guns. The mere sound of them from a nearby hunting lease could evoke flashbacks from Afghanistan that made his palms sweat and his heart race.

Another reason the letter from the historical society had him so flustered. He'd worked for ten years to preserve his quiet way of life out here on the ranch—and now they were telling him this place was one of the original Juniper Bluff homesteads. *And* they were planning a huge sesquicentennial celebration next year and wanted to feature his property on a grand tour.

True, Kent had known the place was a fixer-upper when he bought it—but a hundred and fifty years old? That had come as a surprise. Previous owners over the years had added modern plumbing, wiring and other basic updates. With a few minor repairs now and then to keep the place livable, it had served Kent just fine. He couldn't imagine who'd be interested in touring a run-down old house and barn.

And spending his hard-earned cash to make things presentable for a bunch of gawkers? Uh-uh. Not happening. With fewer and fewer calves being born each year, his ranching account was dropping deeper into the red. If he hoped to keep this dream alive, every penny he could put aside had to go toward a quality registered bull to replace the old fella who'd outlived his productive years.

Thanks to a recent spring storm, though, he'd had no choice but to dip into his savings to repair the leaky barn roof. Last year, it was his septic tank, and the year before, his rattletrap of a truck needed a new timing belt.

Yep, much as he loved ranch life, it was definitely one challenge after another.

He found the strays at the westernmost border of his land. Apparently, they'd discovered a weak spot in one of his pasture fences and wandered down to drink from a burbling creek running deep and fresh from spring rains. He had to do little more than wave his hat, whistle through his teeth and keep centered in the saddle as Jasmine expertly turned the heifers in the direction of home.

Once they'd rejoined the herd, Kent rode the fence line to look for any other sections in need of repair. Finding two more trouble spots, he made quick temporary fixes to hold until he could do the job right tomorrow afternoon after his shift ended at the hardware store. Supplementing with part-time work in town gave him a little extra to live on anyway.

Back at the barn, he unsaddled Jasmine and brushed her down before leading her into her stall. He tossed in a flake of hay, refilled her water pail and dumped a scoop of feed into her tray. The mare gave a nicker of gratitude and settled in for her supper.

Kent chuckled to himself. *He* should have it so easy.

When he walked through his back door and into his empty kitchen a few minutes later, the weight of living alone hit him like a punch to the gut. Which was crazy, because the solitary life was exactly what he wanted— no, *needed*. Peace and quiet and green growing things all around him. And his animals—a trusty cow horse, a couple of gentle mares he'd rescued, a few head of cattle and the sleepy old dog, who on day one of his adoption, had claimed Kent's easy chair and relegated him permanently to the sofa.

"I'm home, Skip." Kent tossed his dusty felt hat onto the breakfast table and stooped to pick up Skip's food dish. "Hungry, boy?"

A thud followed by toenails clicking on hardwood announced the yellow half Lab's lazy approach. Kent filled the dog's dish with kibble, and while Skip munched, Kent's gaze swept the drab walls, bare of any adornments except for the calendar his boss at the hardware store gave out to all his customers every December. The kitchen, like every room in the house—and the outside, too, for that matter—badly needed a fresh coat of paint.

Except for the couple of times a year when his folks

came down from Tulsa for a visit, Kent never much concerned himself with appearances, and why should he start now? Yeah, his mom was always on his case about how the place could sure use a woman's touch. Every visit, she'd get busy cleaning light fixtures and rearranging his badly disorganized cupboards, while Dad puttered around outside, pulling weeds or shoring up sagging porch steps.

But standing here now, and with visions of this afternoon's pretty basket weaver playing through his mind like a video on an endless loop, Kent found himself wondering what Erin Dearborn would have to say about his bleak living conditions. She clearly had an eye for beauty, not to mention a talent for creating art from what anyone else would toss aside. He could still recall the delicate feel of the little twig basket in his hand, still picture the amazingly realistic straw bluebonnets and the dainty letter *A*, so perfectly formed. He wondered what the initial stood for—maybe her daughter's name?

You can ask next time you see her.

Startled by the realization that he *wanted* there to be a next time, Kent pulled a quick breath of air into his lungs. *Seriously?* He was allowing one random encounter to make him question everything about the life he'd so carefully constructed for himself? Kent had long ago decided he wasn't relationship material anyway, not with the baggage he carried from his wartime service as a corpsman.

Nope, this bachelor cowboy had everything he needed right here. He'd stick a frozen dinner in the microwave, and after supper, he'd fall asleep in front of the TV while his dog snored in the easy chair. Tomorrow morning, he'd get up early for chores, work at the hardware store till noon, come home for lunch and then get busy fixing those fences. Routine was his comfort zone, and nobody better mess with it.

Yep, the historical society could just find some other old house to show off.

Chapter Two

"Avery, get a move on. We're running late." Erin scooped up her purse and keys from the kitchen table, then snatched Avery's lunchbox off the counter. "Grab your backpack, honey. And don't forget a sweater."

"I'm hurrying as fast as I can, Mom." Stomping feet echoed from the hallway. "And anyway, you should have woken me up sooner."

Erin pressed the button to open the garage door. "I know, and I'm sorry," she said as Avery bounded past her. "I forgot to set my alarm."

She wasn't sure when it began, this struggle to get anywhere on time. Growing up, she'd earned a reputation for being early to everything. Maybe it was the people pleaser in her, the same part that had kept her married to an abuser in hopes that if she was good enough, if she tried hard enough, she could eventually change him.

Now, with Payne out of the picture, apparently she'd relaxed her standards. Or else it was rebellion, pure and simple. Her way of reclaiming a semblance of control over her life.

Whatever the case, she needed to redevelop the habit of punctuality. Getting her daughter to and from school on time was important, yes, but when Erin reported to her new job at Wanda's Wonders next week, she couldn't expect the gift shop's owner to overlook tardiness.

As she sped through downtown Juniper Bluff toward the school, Avery kicked the seat back. "You're driving too fast, Mom. You're gonna get a ticket."

At that very moment, Erin spotted a patrol car parked where the school zone began. Guiltily, she eased her foot off the accelerator and allowed the car to coast until the speedometer dropped below twenty miles per hour. Pasting on an innocent smile, she steered past the officer and into the school's drop-off lane.

A teacher's aide opened Avery's door, and she scooted out. "Bye, Mom. See you after school!"

Waving to her daughter, Erin swallowed down the lump in her throat. She still couldn't believe her little girl would soon finish first grade. Where had the years gone? This Saturday would be Avery's seventh birthday. Erin still needed to put the finishing touches on the basket she'd started yesterday. It wasn't much of a birthday gift, but for now, it was something Erin could afford. Besides, Avery loved collecting pretty things—beads, rocks, feathers, leaves—and this basket would be a perfect place to keep her treasures.

Before Erin could finish the basket, though, she had another chore on her to-do list. The small three-bedroom bungalow her brother Greg had helped her purchase suited their needs just right, and the neighborhood seemed safe enough. But living on her own for the first time in her life, she couldn't shake her apprehension. Ideally, she'd prefer to install an alarm system—another expense she couldn't afford. Instead, she'd decided to invest in security lights for the front and back of the house. Those shouldn't cost too much, and how hard could they be to install?

Picking up groceries last weekend, Erin had noticed a hardware store across from the supermarket. A few minutes after leaving the school, she pulled into the Zipp's Hardware parking lot and found a space between a dirt-encrusted pickup and an older-model hatchback. The brick building with the green metal sign across the front appeared to have been around almost as long as the town itself. All kinds of intriguing gadgets lined the display windows on either side of the entrance, and Erin grew so entranced that she almost forgot why she'd come—until the door burst open and a crusty old guy in overalls and a baseball cap nearly plowed into her. He mumbled an apology, climbed into the dirty pickup and drove away.

So much for small-town friendliness. With an annoyed shake of her head, Erin marched inside. She paused to get her bearings, her gaze skimming the signage over each aisle: Plumbing, Tools, Fasteners, Electric...

"Can I help you?"

Erin turned with a start. *"You?"*

"You!" yesterday's cowboy said at exactly the same time.

She backed up a step, yesterday's butterflies returning with ferocity. "You work here?"

"I do." One brow arched. "Did you make it on time to pick up your daughter?"

"Yes. I mean, no. But it was okay. She was helping

her teacher feed the gerbils." And *why* did Erin feel the need to explain herself?

The cowboy looked at her askance, one wayward lock of brown hair sliding across his temple. "Gerbils. Aren't those just glorified rats?"

"They're actually pretty cute. I had a pair when I was a kid. And then they had babies and Mom made me give them away—" Lips pursed, Erin crossed her arms. "I—I'm actually looking for security lights. Do you carry those?"

"Lighting's in aisle seven." Starting in that direction, he peered over his shoulder. "Erin, isn't it?"

"Yes," she said, hurrying to follow. "I'm sorry. I'm terrible with names. Ken?"

"Kent." He stopped about halfway down the aisle. "Here we go. Security lights. You want manual or automatic?"

Erin bit her lip. "What's the basic difference?"

Slanting her a crooked smile, Kent picked up a box. "This one's manual. That means you have to turn it on and off yourself from the light switch."

"Of course." With a silly-me eye roll, Erin bent to read the printing on another box. "So…automatic means the lights come on by themselves, obviously. How do they know?" She cringed at how ignorant she must sound.

"Well, there's the kind where you set a timer for exactly when you want the light to go on and off. Then there's this one," he said, indicating the box she was examining, "which has a simple light sensor. On at dusk, off at dawn."

"I like that."

"Or there's one other option," Kent said, reaching

for a box on a higher shelf. "This one has both a light sensor and a motion detector. If you don't want the light on all night, you can set it to come on only when there's activity to trigger it."

Erin hadn't realized she'd have so many choices. An amber warning light blinked in her brain. "That one's probably the most expensive."

"Yeah, they do go up in price when you start getting fancy. Where do you plan to use it?"

"Front and back porches."

"Any reason you wouldn't want the lights on all night? Like bedroom windows nearby, or neighbors who might be annoyed?"

Valid points. Points Erin hadn't considered. "How much exactly is the motion-detector style?"

Kent brought a box down from the shelf. "This one's our bestselling model. It's priced at $69.95." He must have noticed her flinch, because he returned the box to its place and chose another one instead. "Now, this one here has fewer bells and whistles but works just as good, and it's $30 cheaper."

Still a lot, but definitely more affordable. Erin pictured her minuscule checkbook balance. Maybe she could buy one today and hold off on the second one until after she got her first paycheck.

She felt Kent's eyes on her. Thoughtfully, he asked, "You were wanting two, right?" When she replied with a hesitant nod, he drew a hand across his chin. "This is actually a closeout model. With the newer ones expected any day now, we need to clear out shelf space. I'll sell you the second light for half price."

Erin brightened. "Really? That would be great!" If things went well, she could have the lights installed before she picked up Avery from school. And maybe tonight she'd actually get a full night's sleep instead of tossing and turning and listening for every little sound.

What *was* it about this woman? Clenching his teeth, Kent tucked two of the security light kits under his arm and strode toward the cash register. Good thing ol' Ben Zipp, the store's penny-pinching owner, wasn't in this morning. Kent hadn't lied about a newer model coming out—this manufacturer typically updated the line every year—but there'd been no catalog info as yet.

As for the discounted price? Kent would have to ring it up as quoted and then make the correction after Erin left the store. He'd make up the difference out of his own pocket. And maybe settle for PB&J for lunch at home instead of stopping for a sub sandwich at the supermarket deli.

He keyed in the purchase and stated the total. "Cash, check or charge?"

"Check." Erin tugged out her wallet. "I know hardly anybody writes checks anymore, but it helps me keep to my budget."

He understood about tight finances. "No problem, as long as you have some ID."

"Yes, of course." She handed him a check along with her driver's license.

Frowning, Kent compared the information. The driver's license showed a Dallas address, but the check indicated she lived in San Antonio. "Uh, which is it?"

"Oh. Neither." A blush brightened the dusting of freckles across her cheeks. "I used to live in Dallas, but then I moved in with my brother in San Antonio for a short time, and now I live in Juniper Bluff. With my daughter. We just moved here last weekend actually. We're still getting settled."

"I get it. All this changeover stuff takes time." Kent had strict instructions from his boss about check acceptance, though, and conflicting addresses definitely put this one on the questionable list. "Do you have any other form of ID? Something showing your current place of residence would be best."

Erin plopped her purse on the counter and began rummaging through it. "How about this?" She pulled out a creased and crumpled paper, smoothed out the page and turned it to face Kent. "I just got this from the post office confirming my change of address."

"That'll work." Kent entered the payment in the register. While the receipt printed out, he slid the light kits into a large plastic shopping bag. "All set."

"Thanks." Scooping up her purse and the bag, Erin mumbled, "Now I just have to figure out how to install them."

Kent figured he'd regret this, but the look on her pretty elfin face was quickly banishing all reason. "If you need some help, I moonlight as a handyman."

"I'm sure I can manage." Her shaky smile said otherwise. "These come with directions, right? How hard can it be?"

"How much do you know about electric wiring?"

Her shrug said, *Not much.*

"Seriously, I work cheap." *Not really.* He was saving for that bull after all. So why was he going off the rails to help a complete stranger? "My shift ends at noon. Why don't I come by and at least walk you through it? I don't want you getting electrocuted or anything."

At the word *electrocuted*, Erin's face paled. She set

the bag back on the counter. "The thing is, a handyman currently isn't in my budget. If these are that complicated to install, then I should probably—"

"How are you at making sandwiches?"

"What?"

"Sandwiches. Bread, mayo, a slice or two of cold cuts?" He'd kick himself later, but the thought of this tiny woman playing with live electric wires while standing on a wobbly stepladder... Not happening on his watch. "What I'm saying is, I'll trade you an hour or so of security light installation for whatever you've got on hand for lunch."

Lips pressed together, Erin eyed him doubtfully. "You'd actually do that, after I already inconvenienced you by trespassing on your property and requiring a horseback ride to my car?"

"Consider it my way of welcoming a Juniper Bluff newcomer." People had certainly been helpful to Kent when he'd first moved here ten years ago with little more than a dream and his VA loan. Almost everything he knew about cattle ranching he'd learned through the kindness of strangers—a few who had quickly become friends. Thankfully, most didn't seem to mind that he wasn't much of a socializer.

One of the best of them was walking in the door right now. Kent nodded to Seth Austin, part owner and manager of Serenity Hills Guest Ranch. "Be right with you, Seth."

The lanky cowboy tugged off his Stetson and ran a hand through his hair. "No hurry. I'll be over here in Plumbing."

Kent turned back to Erin. "So are we on for lunch?" Yikes, that sounded *way* too much like a date.

"Only if you're sure." She fingered the plastic bag.

"If I wasn't sure, I wouldn't have offered." Truth be told, he wasn't all that sure, but he wouldn't back out now. "Let me see your post office form again so I can get the address."

Once he'd copied the information into his phone, Erin gathered up her purchase. On her way to the door, she thanked him several times and promised to have lunch ready a few minutes after twelve.

Before he forgot, Kent made the adjustments to the sales record and chipped in the difference for the second security light. *Pushover*, his inner voice taunted. He'd have to make up some excuse to explain why part of the purchase was made with a check and the rest in cash.

Ambling down the plumbing aisle, he met up with Seth in front of a bathroom faucet display. "Looking to replace something?"

"Yeah, we're continuing to update cabins." Seth tried the handle of one of the faucets. "So who's your pretty new customer?" he asked with a grin. "And did I actually overhear confirmed bachelor Kent Ritter making a *date*?"

A nervous chuckle rumbled in Kent's throat. "It's not like that. She's just somebody new in town. I'm going to help her install security lights."

"She wouldn't be Greg O'Grady's sister, would she? I heard he bought Diana Matthews's house for her—well, Diana Willoughby now, since she and Tripp got married."

"Wouldn't know. Her name's Erin Dearborn."

"That sounds right. She's had a pretty rough time. Greg's helping her get a new start."

Kent had heard about Greg O'Grady and the San

Antonio charitable organization that hosted the camps at Seth's guest ranch. If Erin was Greg's sister, Kent worried a whole lot less about the risks of accepting her check.

"What kind of a rough time?" he asked.

"Bad marriage, complicated divorce—that's all I know." Seth examined another faucet. "Would you have three of these in stock?"

Kent found two boxes on a lower shelf, then had to run to the back for the third. Seth met him up front at the checkout and added a couple of pipe fittings and a roll of plumber's tape to his purchase. Kent ran Seth's credit card and bagged the items.

Seth slapped on his Stetson. "Pretty clear what I'll be doing the rest of the day."

Guilt niggled at Kent's nape. If he weren't so stubbornly single-minded, he'd be doing some fixing up of his own. "Say," he began, "know anything about this Juniper Bluff sesquicentennial thing?"

"Yeah, they're planning some big doings for next year. My grandparents are on the committee."

"Is your ranch one of the historical sites?"

Chuckling, Seth shook his head. "Serenity Hills has been around awhile, but not a hundred and fifty years. Which is too bad, because being declared a historical site means a sizable discount on property taxes." He cocked his head. "Hey, you own the old Gilliam place. Have you checked to see if it qualifies?"

"I, uh…heard it might." Tax savings? Yep, this definitely bore looking into. "Any problems with those faucets, let me know."

"Thanks." Seth winked as he picked up his purchases. "Gotta get going. You have a nice lunch date with Erin."

"It's not a—"

Too late. Seth had already breezed out the door.

At five minutes after twelve, Kent climbed into his grimy tan pickup parked behind the store. With only two more customers after Seth left, the morning had crept by, which meant Kent had plenty of time to mull over Seth's parting words: *sizable discount on property taxes.* How could he turn up his nose at anything that could help him keep the ranch going? Sesquicentennial tour? Bring it on.

On the other hand, fixing up the place wouldn't be cheap, and then he'd have to deal with all those people traipsing through his house. Maybe not such a great trade-off after all.

Yep, he needed to think on this awhile.

And then there was Erin Dearborn, yet another disruption, albeit a pretty one, to his comfortable, quiet life. Sooner than he was prepared for, he pulled into her driveway. The garage door stood open, and a blue Camry sat inside, the trunk lid raised. As he stepped from the pickup, he glimpsed several cardboard boxes in the trunk.

The house door opened, and Erin appeared alongside the car. "Oh, you're here already. Sorry, I was just moving in a few more of my things."

"You say that a lot," Kent observed, striding toward her.

She cast him a questioning frown. "What, that I'm still moving in?"

"No, that you're sorry. It's okay. You don't have to apologize all the time."

"I didn't realize I did that. I'm sor—" She stopped

herself with a hand to her lips, and for a moment Kent thought she might start crying. Then a strangled chuckle burst from her throat. Blue eyes twinkling, she hiked her chin. "In that case, I'm *not* sorry. Not one bit."

Kent grinned. Did she have any idea how irresistible that smile was? Except he had every intention of resisting. How many times did he have to remind himself this wasn't a social call? He nodded toward the trunk. "All these go inside?"

"Yes, but I'll get them later. You're probably ready for lunch, and I'm sure you'd rather get started with those lights so you can be on your way."

"No hurry," Kent heard himself saying, as if a complete stranger had taken over his body. He hefted one of the boxes from the trunk, only to risk his knees buckling at the unexpected weight. "What's in here—boulders for your rock collection?"

Erin reached out to steady the load. "Oh, sorry—I mean—"

Kent felt downright sorry to think Erin's lousy marriage could be the reason she seemed so unsure of herself. "It's okay. Just show me where you want this."

With a tight nod, she spun around and held the door for him. They stepped into a brightly lit kitchen, and he followed her into the adjoining family room.

She motioned toward a half-filled bookcase. "That's more books, so right here on the floor is fine."

The box hit the floor with a thud. How in the world had a petite woman like Erin figured to lift a box that heavy by herself? Kent straightened to ease his back. "Why don't you get started on lunch while I bring in the rest of those boxes?"

Before she could protest, Kent shot her a noarguments smile and tramped back out to the garage. By the time he'd carried in the last of her packed belongings, the savory aromas of tomato soup and grilled cheese sandwiches had him salivating. Erin directed him to the powder room so he could wash up, and when he returned to the kitchen, she'd set two places for them at a small dinette.

"Fancy," Kent murmured as he took in the teal straw place mats, napkins folded just so and the sandwiches cut into four neat triangles surrounding each soup bowl. An intricately woven twig basket, slightly larger than the one he'd seen her making yesterday, graced the center of the table and held an assortment of fresh fruit.

Erin gripped one of the chair backs. "Did I forget anything? Would you rather have something besides water to drink?"

"Water's fine. And it all looks great." Amazing, in fact. Unaccustomed to dining in such style, Kent had the sudden urge to do the gentlemanly thing and get Erin's chair for her.

She didn't give him the chance. Scooting into the seat, she motioned for him to do the same. "Would you like to say grace?"

"I, uh…" Kent swallowed something hard in his throat. Probably a chunk of his hardened heart, the result of seeing too much action in Afghanistan.

"I understand if you'd rather not." She smiled as she smoothed her napkin across her lap. "Please, go ahead and eat."

As he picked up a sandwich triangle, Erin dipped her chin, eyes closed in a moment of silence. He waited respectfully until she looked up. "My turn to apologize," he murmured. "It's been a long time since I did any praying."

"It's okay. 'Called or not called, God is present.'" Erin dipped her spoon into her soup and blew gently across the surface.

Kent pondered the words as he took another bite of his sandwich. "Is that a quote from somebody?"

"I don't know the source, but it's always given me comfort." Her gaze shifted toward the window. "There have been plenty of times when I doubted God's presence. It's reassuring to know His love and constancy don't depend on my belief."

Something else Kent would have to think on for a while. But not today. Best to get through this meal, take care of those security lights and head for home. He still had fences to fix and cattle to tend—things that made sense to him, unlike God and women and anything else that threatened his safe little world.

Bracing the stepladder with one hand, Erin passed Kent a screwdriver. After a few quick turns, he had the second of the security lights installed, this one over the backyard patio. Before they began, Erin had glanced at the directions. If she had tried to install the lights on her own, she'd still be at step one and utterly confused.

"Almost done," Kent said. "Pass me up the bulbs and we'll make sure everything's working."

Erin reached into the box at her feet and handed him the floodlight bulbs one at a time. Once he'd screwed them in, he gave her the go-ahead to flip the switch at the breaker box. By the time she returned from the garage, Kent had his tools packed up and the ladder folded.

"Working fine," he said. "I've set the detection zones

for both the front and rear fixtures. After it gets dark, anything larger than your neighbor's cat should trigger the sensor and turn on the lights. Any problems, let me know and I'll come back to make some adjustments."

"Thank you. Really, thank you so much." Erin walked with him around the side of the house to his pickup. As he shoved his toolbox into the space behind the driver's seat, she said, "Please let me pay you something, though. Lunch hardly seems like a fair trade."

"Are you kidding?" Kent laughed in a way that made her insides all tingly. "Haven't eaten so fancy since my last trip home when my mom cooked for me."

"Where's home?" Erin asked, realizing she wasn't particularly anxious for him to leave.

"Tulsa, Oklahoma. My dad has a car dealership there." Hefting the stepladder, Kent moved around to the pickup bed and laid it inside.

Admiring the way his biceps flexed beneath the sleeves of his Zipp's Hardware polo shirt, Erin gave herself a mental shake. "Never been to Tulsa. Is it nice?"

"Pretty country, if you can stand the blazing summers and the likelihood of winter ice storms or the occasional blizzard."

"Is the weather why you moved to Texas?"

A faraway look in his eyes, Kent braced one hip against the side of the truck. "Just always wanted to go into ranching, and when I found the right place at the right price… Well, here I am." With a smirk, he pivoted to climb in behind the wheel. "And now I'm off to work my cattle. Like I said, call if you have any problems."

Watching him drive away, Erin sighed as she fingered the Zipp's Hardware business card he'd given her after jotting his personal cell phone number on the back. She liked Kent Ritter. Liked him a lot. If a man as nice as Kent had come along before she'd met Payne, her life could have turned out a whole lot differently.

Maybe.

Or maybe not. Because she'd had a lot of growing up to do since then, and still had a ways to go. Kent's words from earlier this afternoon played through her thoughts. *You don't have to apologize all the time.* That was the people-pleaser side of her again, making her think the only way to be liked or accepted—or *loved*— was to continually put others' needs before her own.

But wasn't that biblical? Paul wrote in Romans that Christians mustn't think more highly of themselves than they ought, being kind to one another and putting others first. Jesus Himself said, *But I say unto you, That ye resist not evil: but whosoever shall smite thee on thy right cheek, turn to him the other also.*

Instinctively, Erin's hand went to her cheek. She could still feel the sting of the last time Payne had slapped her. Her breath quickened. Her heart slammed against her breastbone.

Never again.

Chapter Three

For the first couple of nights after getting the new security lights installed, Erin slept even worse than she had without them. It was no longer only unfamiliar noises that disturbed her sleep, but the need to peek out the window every hour or two to check if the lights had come on. So far, they hadn't, which made her question whether she should call Kent and have him double-check the detection sensitivity.

No, she was a big girl now. She ought to be perfectly capable of digging those instructions out of the drawer where she'd stashed them and figuring out how to make adjustments all on her own. Besides, spending more time than necessary with the good-looking cowboy-slash-handyman could prove risky. She should know from experience how susceptible she was to the kind attentions of a handsome man.

A man who'd plainly admitted he wasn't on speaking terms with the Lord and might just as easily be hiding a cruel streak as bad as Payne's.

Except those lighting instructions were *so* intimidating, and Erin's artistic right-brain intelligence didn't play well with left-brain details. She'd give it one more night, and if she still had doubts that the lights were adjusted properly, she'd *consider* calling Kent.

Then in the wee hours of Saturday morning, Erin opened her eyes to a bright white glow and strange snuffling and scratching sounds outside her bedroom window. Heart hammering, she tossed back the covers and grabbed her dad's old nine iron from under the bed. With the golf club clutched firmly in one hand, she used the fingers of the other to separate two of the mini-blind slats.

When she peered out, a startled gasp froze in her throat. A small herd of deer ambled through her front yard, two of them pausing to nibble in the flower bed closest to the house. Erin hadn't had a chance to do any weeding or planting yet, but she'd noticed a few stray hostas poking up through the mulch. Since the deer obviously considered them delicacies, Erin might have to do some research on deer-resistant plants.

"Mommy?" Rubbing her eyes, Avery tottered into the room. "It's so light. Is it morning already?"

"Not yet, honey, but come and see." Erin found the cord and raised the blinds an inch or two above the sill. Then she knelt on the carpet and drew her daughter to her side. "Look—deer!"

Avery sucked in an excited breath, her dainty fingers grasping the sill as she leaned closer to the window. "They're so pretty! I didn't know we would have deer at our new house."

"Me, neither." Guess Erin had a lot of new experiences to look forward to in the Hill Country.

Avery shivered with happiness. "Maybe God sent them just for me, 'cause today's my birthday."

"Maybe He did, honey." Erin gave her little girl a squeeze. Avery's childlike faith in God's loving kindness was a constant inspiration to Erin, especially when circumstances challenged her own faith.

They watched in silence until the deer moved on and the security lights blinked off. Yawning, Avery hugged her mother's neck. "I'm still sleepy. Can I snuggle with you till morning?"

"Absolutely."

With her head nestled against Erin's shoulder and the covers tucked in all around them, Avery's breathing soon slowed into the rhythm of sound sleep. For Erin, though, it was hopeless. For the next hour, she lay there staring into the darkness and pondering her future.

Never in a million years had she imagined herself starting over as a single mom—worse, a single mom dependent on her older brother for the very roof over their heads. Even though Greg was a widower and his daughter was away at college most of the year, she'd known she and Avery couldn't expect to share his San Antonio condo indefinitely. Still, when he'd suggested this move to Juniper Bluff, she'd voiced her doubts. But he'd been so persuasive in describing the small town, friendly neighbors, a good school where Avery could make new friends. He'd promised a peaceful haven where Erin could begin to heal from the wounds of her abusive marriage, and she offered a silent prayer that his words would prove true.

Just when she'd finally dozed off, Avery bolted upright and jiggled her mother's arm. "Mommy, wake up. My birthday's here. I'm seven now!"

"Yes, you are." Stretching, Erin smiled up at her little

girl. "Guess we'd better start celebrating. What would you like for breakfast?"

"Heart-shaped pancakes with chocolate chips."

Anticipating her daughter's request, Erin had picked up the ingredients yesterday at the supermarket. She crawled out of bed and shooed Avery to her room to get dressed, then pulled on a long-sleeved T-shirt and a pair of jeans before tromping barefoot to the kitchen.

When she reached into the cupboard for the pancake mix, the shelf gave way and everything on it tumbled onto the counter and then to the floor. The box of pancake mix split open, surrounding Erin in a floury dust cloud.

"Are you *kidding*?" Ten or fifteen dollars' worth of groceries lay strewed around her feet. She lifted her hands in dismay.

Avery rushed into the kitchen. "Mommy, what happened?"

"Stay back, sweetie. Mommy had a little accident." Erin didn't see any broken glass, thank goodness, but she didn't need Avery tracking through the mess.

Crouching down for a better look, Avery frowned. "Uh-oh. Now we can't make my pancakes."

"We'll figure something else out." One giant step took Erin out of ground zero. She turned to survey the damage while racking her brain for a way to salvage Avery's birthday breakfast. "Since we can't do pancakes, what would you say to breakfast at the doughnut shop? Remember how good those crullers were when we had them with Uncle Greg on moving day?"

Avery jumped at the idea. As soon as Erin changed out of her pancake-mix-spattered clothes, they hopped in the car. A few minutes later, Erin parked on the town square in front of Diana's Donuts.

Diana Willoughby welcomed them at the counter. "Hi, Erin. How are things at the house?"

Rather than admit to the former owner that Erin was already dealing with repair issues, she smiled and said, "Fine. We love our new home."

"We had deer in our yard last night," Avery piped up. "It was God's birthday present for me."

Diana rested her elbows on the counter to smile at Avery. "Wow, cool!"

"But then the shelf broke—"

Erin cringed.

"—so we couldn't make my birthday pancakes and Mommy said we could have breakfast here."

"Oh, no." Diana cast Erin an apologetic frown. "The cupboard nearest the refrigerator? I should have warned you about that shelf. I've had problems before."

"Please don't worry about it," Erin said with a shrug. "Things happen."

Brightening, Diana looked past Erin's shoulder. "And here's my go-to guy for when *things happen*. Hi, Kent. Let me introduce you to someone."

Erin whirled around to see Kent Ritter ambling over. He palmed his hat, allowing a stray coffee-colored curl to dip across his brow. "We've met, actually," he said with a nod to Erin. "Lights working okay?"

"Seem to be." Coffee. Erin needed coffee. Anything to ease the sudden dryness in her throat. Aware of her daughter moving between her and Kent, she settled her hands on Avery's stiff shoulders.

Kent glanced down, his lips twitching into a hesitant half smile. "This your daughter?"

Erin nodded. "Avery, this is Mr. Ritter, the nice man who installed our new lights."

It felt as if Avery grew two inches. Her normally sweet voice hardened. "You were at our house?"

"Uh, yes." Edging back a step, Kent shot Erin a questioning look.

"It's okay, honey." Erin gave her daughter's shoulders a reassuring squeeze. In the last couple of years leading up to the divorce, and especially in the months since then, she'd noticed Avery's tension around certain men. Could Erin ever forgive herself for the collateral damage Payne's spousal abuse had inflicted on their daughter? She should have gotten out sooner.

Diana cleared her throat. "Excuse me, but the line's growing. Did y'all want to order something?"

"Oh, sorry." Hearing the apology leave her lips, Erin caught the subtle lift of Kent's right eyebrow. She turned to Diana. "We'd like one coffee, one milk and…"

"Can I have an apple fritter, Mommy?"

"That sounds good. Make it two." Erin fumbled for her wallet. Discovering she was down to only three dollars in cash, she pulled her lower lip between her teeth. "I don't suppose you'd take a check?"

Diana hesitated a split second too long. "From you? Sure."

"No need for that." Kent stepped up to the counter. "Didn't I hear it's this little lady's birthday? Let this be my treat."

"I couldn't." Erin firmly shook her head.

"Please, I'd like to do this." Kent already had his billfold out. He smiled at Erin in a way that suggested he was all too aware of her unfortunate circumstances. "And over breakfast you can tell me more about this broken shelf."

* * *

When Kent had first walked into the doughnut shop, buying breakfast for Erin and her daughter had been the furthest thing from his mind. He'd just picked up a few supplies at the feed store and only thought to grab a quick cup of coffee and one of those delicious blueberry scones Diana's assistant, Kimberly, was noted for.

Now, instead of heading straight home to ranch chores, here he sat with his coffee and scone across from a nervous-looking Erin and a little girl whose direct gaze held both suspicion and a clear warning to keep his distance. Kent hadn't spent much time around kids, but he knew enough to realize Avery Dearborn was too young to feel this protective of her mother.

"Really, you didn't have to do this," Erin said as she nibbled on her fritter. "Please, let me pay you back."

"Not necessary." Best to nip this line of conversation in the bud. "So what happened with the shelf?"

Erin hiked a shoulder. "I barely touched it. Next thing I knew, everything was on the floor."

"I've got time to take a look." Kent winced inwardly. He still had a day's worth of chores ahead of him. Besides, did he dare involve himself in Erin's life any more than he already had?

"My mom can fix it," Avery said with a thrust of her chin. She flicked a flake of fritter glaze from the corner of her mouth. "Anyways, I'm seven now. I can help her."

"I'm sure you can." Kent shared a brief smile with Erin. "But since it's your birthday, I figured you already had some fun plans for the day."

Eyes lowered, Avery toyed with her fork. "I guess so."

The regretful look clouding Erin's expression stabbed

Kent's heart. "We haven't been settled long enough to plan a party."

Kent gave a solemn nod. "A birthday without a party. Doesn't get much worse than that." He took a slow sip of coffee and realized he was about to get even more involved in the lives of Erin Dearborn and her daughter. Resting a forearm on the table, he fixed Avery with a thoughtful frown. "Ever been on a horseback ride?"

The girl's head shot up, interest sparking in eyes the same shade of crystal blue as her mother's. "My cousin has a horse. She let me ride with her once. But only around the corral. And she wouldn't trot or gallop or anything."

"That takes all the fun out of it, huh?" Kent winked at Erin.

An endearing blush crept up her cheeks. Her darting glance suggested she hadn't told Avery about her ride on Jasmine the other day. "Finish your milk, honey. We should get home and clean up our mess."

"I'm serious about taking a look at the shelf," Kent said as he pushed away from the table. "And I was serious about a horseback ride, too—if you're interested, that is."

Lips pursed, Erin turned to her daughter. "It's your birthday, sweetie. What do you think?"

"I'd like to, but…" Indecision played across Avery's heart-shaped face. Her narrowed gaze landed on Kent, and she folded her arms, signaling a clear *no*.

Tough audience. Not that Kent could blame the kid. She didn't know Kent and had no reason to trust him. "That's okay," he said. "Maybe some other time."

"I'm sorry—" Erin began.

Kent cut her off with a jerk of his chin, tempered

with a friendly smile. Rising, he set his hat firmly on his head. "If y'all are headed straight home, I'll follow you over. We'll get that shelf fixed lickety-split, and then you'll have the rest of the day to do whatever the birthday girl wants."

With a quiet thank-you, Erin gathered her purse and guided Avery to the door. A few minutes later, Kent pulled in behind them in Erin's driveway. By the time he strode in through the garage with his toolbox, Erin was already at work with a broom and dustpan, while Avery collected canned goods and other odds and ends that must have been on the shelf.

Erin glanced up at Kent with a nervous smile. "I told you it was a mess."

"She didn't mean to," Avery asserted. She slammed two cans of beans onto the counter. "It was an accident."

"Avery, watch your tone." Another embarrassed *I'm sorry* flitted across Erin's face.

Before the words found her tongue, Kent barked out a quick laugh. "You ever see a fifty-pound sack of grain bust open in the middle of the barn? Now, *that's* a mess." After setting his toolbox and hat on the counter, he edged around Erin to take a closer look at the cupboard and shelf. "Yep, here's the problem right here."

"You figured it out already?" Erin emptied her dustpan into the trash can under the sink, then strode over.

He showed her where one of the metal shelf pins was loose. "It's like a table with a wobbly leg. If things aren't balanced exactly right, the whole thing tips over."

"How hard will it be to fix?"

"This hole where the pin goes has gotten reamed out. A little wood filler should do the trick." Kent lifted the top tray of his toolbox and poked around beneath for a small plastic container. Using a putty knife, he applied wood filler to the hole and then inserted the pin, making sure it was level.

The whole time he worked, he sensed Erin watching over his shoulder. "That looked too easy." She sounded miffed. "I should have been able to fix it myself."

"Maybe, after you made a trip to the hardware store for the right supplies. And then you'd be stuck with most of a can of wood filler that you might never use again."

"You have a point." Arms crossed, Erin stepped closer to examine Kent's repair. The fresh scent of jasmine wafted toward him.

Momentarily disconcerted, he put another few inches between them and began packing away his tools. "You should give the filler a few hours to set before you put the shelf back in."

He turned to find Avery studying him, her mouth in a disapproving twist. The concern lurking behind those intense blue eyes felt like a knife to his heart. The last time he'd seen an expression like that on a child's face had been in Afghanistan when he administered medical aid to a village woman hit by a stray bullet during a firefight. The woman's young son, not much older than Avery, had watched every move Kent made. If she died, Kent would be blamed and the boy would lose any trust he had in American servicemen. He'd become an easy target for the Taliban's recruiting efforts to be used as a spy—or worse, a suicide bomber.

Kent had prayed like crazy that day. Prayed for all he was worth. And God hadn't listened.

He hefted the toolbox off the counter and palmed the crown of his hat. "That'll do it, then," he mumbled, sidling toward the door.

"Kent?" Erin caught up as he reached his pickup. "You haven't said what I owe you."

"Nothing. Not a thing." He stowed the toolbox, then forced himself to meet her gaze with a brief smile before climbing in behind the wheel. "You have a good day with the birthday girl."

He needed to get out of here fast, before the memories chewed a hole in his gut. Crazy how such a look in an innocent little girl's eyes could bring it all back so quickly.

What just happened? Erin stared in confusion as Kent sped away. One minute, he'd been making pleasant conversation while finishing up with the shelf and the next, he couldn't seem to escape fast enough.

She marched back inside, where she found Avery sitting cross-legged on the sofa and watching an animal show on TV. Snatching up the remote, Erin hit the off button.

"Mom! I was watching."

"Sorry, but—" She winced, picturing Kent's expression every time she started to apologize. She circled the coffee table to sit down facing her daughter. "Honey, I'm worried something we might have said or done hurt Mr. Ritter's feelings. Can you think of anything?"

Avoiding Erin's gaze, Avery pressed her lips together. "No."

"I couldn't help noticing you weren't very nice to him, either at the doughnut shop or after we got home." Erin lightly touched her daughter's arm. "Want to tell me why?"

Avery responded with an exaggerated shrug. "I

didn't want him to come over. Why couldn't you let Uncle Greg fix the shelf?"

"Uncle Greg can't drop everything to drive over from San Antonio every time we need a little help."

"You could have waited till he comes for Camp Serenity next Friday."

Drawing her daughter into a hug, Erin kissed the top of her head. "Uncle Greg's going to be very busy with the campers. But I promise, if there's a *small* job I need help with that won't take too much time, I'll save it for him."

"Okay." The tension slowly ebbed from Avery's shoulders. "Can we do something fun for my birthday now?"

"Of course. Any ideas?"

Avery heaved a sigh, her lower lip poking out in a pout. Almost under her breath, she said, "If I had a pony like Eva does, I could go on a ride."

Erin had to bite her tongue to keep from reminding her daughter she'd already turned down an offer to go horseback riding. Trying for a lighthearted tone, she quipped, "Our backyard's a little small for a pony, don't you think? I do have a birthday present for you, though. Be right back."

Making a quick trip to her bedroom, Erin returned with the basket she'd wrapped in tissue paper and hidden on the top shelf of her closet. She presented it to her daughter and watched eagerly as Avery tore away the paper.

"Mommy, it's so pretty!" Avery threw one arm around Erin's neck as she admired the little basket. "It even has an *A* for *Avery* on the side."

"I know it isn't a pony," Erin said, hearing the apology creeping into her tone. "But I thought you could use it for some of your treasures."

"I will. Thank you!" Turning to her mother, Avery grew somber. "It's okay that you can't buy me a pony, Mom."

Erin blinked as unexpected tears formed. She gave her daughter another hug while silently vowing that Avery's next birthday would be a much happier occasion.

The ringing of Erin's cell phone interrupted the hug. She hurried to the kitchen counter where she'd left her purse and retrieved the phone. "Hello?"

"Hi, Erin. Your brother Greg gave me your number. We haven't met yet, but our daughters are already best friends." The caller identified herself as Christina Austin, Eva's stepmom. "Eva mentioned today is Avery's birthday. I was thinking, since you've just moved in, you might not have had time to make special plans."

"You're right, we haven't."

"In that case, Eva would love for Avery to come out to the ranch for a playdate. The girls could even go on a pony ride—wearing helmets and totally supervised, of course."

Erin beamed a smile toward her daughter and gave the thumbs-up sign. "Avery would absolutely love it. Thank you so much."

Christina suggested two o'clock and gave Erin directions to the ranch. When Erin shared the invitation with Avery, the little girl squealed and bounced on her toes. "Yay—the best birthday ever!"

While Eva Austin's father accompanied the children on a trail ride, Erin enjoyed coffee and brownies in the ranch kitchen with Christina. She'd had a quick peek at Christina's infant twins as they napped in the nursery upstairs, their sweet faces evoking a pang of longing. She'd always hoped to give Avery a little brother or sister, but that was before Payne's cruelty stole any desire to have more children with him. Until Avery came along, his abuse had been mainly verbal, with an occasional shove or squeeze of Erin's arm. Not long afterward, though, Payne had given Erin her first black eye. He'd blamed the stress of work and having a new baby in the house and apologized profusely. He'd also promised it would never happen again—a promise he had repeatedly failed to keep.

A nudge against Erin's leg drew her attention to the golden retriever who'd just plopped down beside her chair. "Well, hello there."

Christina laughed softly and shook her head. "Gracie, you're supposed to be on your doggy bed."

"Oh, she's okay." Giving the dog a scratch behind the ears, Erin couldn't seem to tear her gaze away from those big brown eyes.

"Gracie's my service dog," Christina said softly. "I was in a bad car accident a few years ago and had a brain injury."

"How awful."

"I'm doing much better now, no small thanks to Gracie." A tender smile warmed Christina's face as she gazed at her dog. "Gracie always seems to know when someone needs a little TLC."

Feeling exposed, Erin gave the dog a final pat and sat up straighter. "Maybe she's picking up on the fact that I'm new in town and not feeling very settled yet."

"Starting over is hard, I know." Christina stirred more cream into her coffee. "We've gotten to know

Greg pretty well over the past several months. He's told us a little about the rough time you've had."

"I don't know how I'd have survived without my brother's support. He even found a part-time job for me at a gift shop in town, Wanda's Wonders." Erin blew out a noisy sigh. "He's hoping I'll be inspired to pursue the career goal I put on hold when I got married."

"Really? What was it?"

"Interior design. My mom had a successful business, and I'd always thought we'd work together someday... until she passed away right after I started college."

"I'm so sorry." Patting Erin's hand, Christina offered a bright smile. "But it's never too late—take my word for it. God has a way of reshaping lost dreams into something even better than we could ever have planned for ourselves."

"I hope you're right."

The back door flew open, and Avery burst in with Eva and her older brother, Joseph. "Mom," Avery gushed, "it was so fun! You should've come with us."

"That's okay," Erin said with an uneasy chuckle. The memory of her wild ride on Kent Ritter's horse was still too fresh. She swiped a stray lock of hair off Avery's forehead, now damp where she'd perspired beneath the riding helmet. "I'm perfectly fine with you being the equestrian of the family."

Christina's husband, Seth, strode into the kitchen. "For a greenhorn, your little girl's pretty good in the saddle. Anytime you're interested in signing her up for riding lessons, let me know."

"Thanks, I'll keep it in mind."

"Hey, hon," Christina said, tugging on Seth's arm. "Did you know Erin studied to be an interior designer?

Maybe she could give us some suggestions for the cabin updates."

Erin blinked. "I don't know—those college classes were a long time ago."

"Please," Christina urged. "Seth doesn't have an artistic bone in his body, and I'm not much better. You could think of it as a stepping stone toward reclaiming your dream career."

A tingle of anticipation warmed Erin's chest. "Well... I suppose I could take a look."

"Wonderful. Do you have time now?"

Checking her watch, Erin decided she could spare a few minutes. While the children played in the backyard, Seth and Christina walked her out to the nearest cabin. As soon as she entered, her brain began buzzing—gingham window curtains with matching throw pillows for the bed, country folk art for the walls, coordinating accessories for the kitchenette and bathroom...

Overwhelmed by the surprising rush of ideas, she paused for breath before sharing her thoughts. Christina's approving nods encouraged her, and she said, "I'd be happy to shop with you one day soon and help you pick out a few things."

"I'd love it. Let me know when you're free."

Stepping from the cabin, she thanked the Austins again for inviting Avery out to ride, then called her daughter to the car.

The second they were on the road, Avery poked the back of Erin's seat. "Mom, can I have riding lessons from Mr. Austin? Please?"

Her mind still humming with decorating ideas, Erin struggled to switch gears. How to explain to an excited birthday girl that riding lessons weren't in the budget?

"Maybe someday, honey, after things ease up a bit and I can save some money."

She still felt bad that Kent had rushed off this morning before she could pay him something for fixing the shelf. Approaching the next crossroads, she remembered turning south here when she'd gone on her basketry materials expedition and ended up on Kent's property. On a whim, she slowed and flipped her turn signal. Somehow, she'd corner Kent Ritter and insist he accept her check, trivial as the amount might be.

"This isn't the way home, Mom," Avery said from the back seat.

"I know, honey. We have a stop to make first."

Erin followed the winding road until she spied Kent's weathered farmhouse on the right. As she turned up the gravel driveway, her tires rattled over the cattle guard. She recognized Kent's pickup parked next to the barn and hoped he was home and not somewhere out in the pasture.

On second thought, if he wasn't around, she could leave her check inside his truck and slip away unnoticed, thus precluding any argument on his part. Yes, she thought with a glance at Avery through the rearview mirror, avoiding confrontation would be ideal.

Then Kent Ritter walked out of the barn.

Chapter Four

Finding Erin Dearborn's little blue sedan parked outside his barn, Kent was temporarily dazed. Tipping back his hat, he strode around to her door and waited while she stepped from the car.

"Um, hi," she said, reaching across the console for her purse. A second later, she had her checkbook open on the hood of the car. "I was driving by and felt I had to stop and pay you something for your trouble this morning. I won't take no for an answer."

Driving by? Kent's place wasn't exactly on the way to anywhere. He glanced in the back seat, where Erin's daughter sat buckled into a booster seat. The look on her tiny face spoke surprise, confusion and no small amount of consternation.

Kent was more than a little confused, as well. A few hours of hard work had helped him pull himself together after his abrupt departure earlier, but he wasn't anxious for a possible replay. "Erin, I told you, I don't need your money. It was a small job, and I was glad to help."

She tore out the check and thrust it into his hand. "I appreciate your kindness, but you were out both supplies and time. Besides, I don't feel comfortable owing anyone—"

"You don't *owe* me anything." Indignation swelling his chest, Kent methodically ripped the check into eight ragged scraps. "I don't know how y'all did things in the big city where you came from, but here in Juniper Bluff, we're all just neighbors helping neighbors."

Erin started to say something, then snapped her mouth closed before trying again. "But neighbors have to make a living, too, don't they?"

Avery had gotten unbuckled and climbed from the back seat. She tucked her hand into her mother's and glared up at Kent.

Time to defuse this tense situation. Palm raised in a placating gesture, Kent eased back a step and tried for a friendly chuckle. "Can we start over here? Look, Erin, I understand things have been tough for you—"

"I *wish* people would stop saying that." She heaved a ragged breath. "It's not like I need to be reminded every five minutes."

"Sorry, I only meant—"

An accusatory smirk skewed Erin's lips. "Now who's apologizing?"

Kent froze, unsure where this was going.

Erin snickered, barely audible at first. "Sorry, I couldn't resist." She glanced down at Avery, and the chuckles grew louder. It was contagious, and now Kent held back laughter.

"Mo-om." The little girl shifted her stern gaze from her mother to Kent and back again. "Why are you laughing?"

"Oh, honey, I'm not sure I can explain." Erin's blue eyes sparkled in the late-afternoon sun, and Kent found himself riveted.

His chuckling stilled. He cleared his throat roughly. At the same time, Erin brought her laughter under control. With a slow and purposeful inhalation, she said, "You're right. We need to start over. Thank you for fixing our shelf, Mr. Ritter. It was very…*neighborly* of you."

"Pleasure's all mine, *neighbor.*" Grinning, he offered his hand to shake, and when Erin took it, he winked and passed her the shredded check.

With a nervous smile, she withdrew her hand and pocketed the scraps.

Just then, loud neighing and a couple of sharp kicks sounded from inside the barn. Kent straightened his hat. "That would be my girls letting me know it's supper time."

Interest shone in Avery's eyes. "Horses?"

"Yup." This might be Kent's opportunity to get on the young lady's good side. "Would you like to meet 'em?"

Avery cast her mother a questioning look, and Erin nodded.

Kent gestured toward the barn. "Okay, then. Right this way."

Before they'd taken three steps, Avery was bubbling over with a description of her pony ride with Eva Austin. "Mr. Austin even let us trot a little bit. It was so bumpy, but I held on tight. Mom said I might be able to have riding lessons after she saves some money from her new job."

"That's terrific." Kent led them over to Jasmine's stall as the big black mare dropped her head over the gate. "I'll be back in a minute with her supper. You can scratch her nose, but don't get too close to her mouth."

By the time he returned with a bucket of grain, Avery

had made fast friends with Jasmine. Erin remained a few paces back, arms folded and a wary look on her face.

"She looks even bigger in her stall," Erin murmured. "But she's beautiful."

As soon as Kent poured a scoop of grain into Jasmine's feed bucket, the horse lost all interest in human attention and turned aside to eat. Kent motioned Erin and her daughter farther along the barn aisle. "Come say hi to Posey and Petunia."

Avery gave a surprised gasp. "You have three horses?"

"I do."

Kent poured grain for Posey, the sorrel mare in the next stall, and she nickered her thanks before burying her nose in the feed bucket. Across the aisle, Posey's sister, Petunia, gave her stall door another kick.

"Comin', girl. Hold your horses."

"That's silly," Avery said as she followed Kent to Petunia's stall. "Horses can't hold their horses."

Erin stood unmoving in the center of the aisle. "It's just an expression, honey. Anyway, we should be going. I'm sure Mr. Ritter has lots to do."

"If Avery wants to stick around for chores, it's fine with me." Even as the words left Kent's mouth, he wondered what alien had taken over his body, because nobody had ever accused him of being Mr. Hospitality. Then he heard himself saying, "After we finish up, I can introduce you to Skip, my dog."

Excitement sparked in Avery's eyes. "Mom—"

"No, honey. You've had plenty of time with horses and dogs today. Now, we really have to go." An edge had crept into Erin's tone, and Kent couldn't tell if it was from her uneasiness around animals or...him.

"Better do what your mom says," Kent said with a quick pat on Avery's shoulder. "Come back anytime, though. Next time I'll show you my cows." He couldn't resist winking at Erin. "Your mom's already met them."

The protective look, one Kent had quickly come to recognize, narrowed Avery's eyes once more. "Mom? You came here a different day?"

"Just once, honey." Erin shot Kent a pointed glare before beaming a smile toward her daughter. "Mr. Ritter was kind enough to let me gather a few supplies to make your birthday basket."

Kent fought a grin. He could still picture Erin's reaction, first when he'd suggested the ride on Jasmine, even more so when he'd mentioned the rattlesnakes. "Have your mom tell you all about it one of these days."

"On that note, we definitely must be on our way." Swiveling toward the exit, Erin stretched out a hand to Avery.

Watching them drive away, Kent suffered another unwelcome pang of loneliness, the kind he'd studiously tamped down ever since Afghanistan. As a navy corpsman assigned to a marine unit, he'd learned it wasn't smart to get too close to anyone, because you never knew if the next mission could mean the last time you saw your friends alive.

But no doubt about it, something about Erin Dearborn had grabbed him by the heart, the first woman to do so since before he'd enlisted. He'd been in love once, but his girlfriend had ended things one week before he left on his second deployment.

"I can't do this again," she'd told him. "Being without you for so long, every day waiting to hear from you, wondering if you're safe—it's too hard."

By the time he returned to civilian life after his third and final deployment, she was married with two kids. Kent figured it was just as well, because by then he'd patched up too many broken bodies and sent too many comrades home beneath flag-draped coffins—so many that some days the shroud of those wartime memories obliterated every shred of daylight to his battered spirit.

Picturing Erin as he'd come upon her on Wednesday beneath the oak tree, sunbeams reaching down through the leaves to spark her auburn hair with golden high-lights, Kent realized he'd seen daylight—really *seen* it—for the first time in forever.

At Christina Austin's suggestion, Erin decided to visit Shepherd of the Hills for Sunday worship. Christina and her grandmother-in-law Marie Peterson, along with the two older Austin children, met Erin and Avery as they entered the foyer.

"Glad you decided to come," Christina said, the sweet service dog, Gracie, close at her side. "Eva can show Avery to their Sunday school class. Marie and I attend the women's Bible study, if you'd like to join us."

Before Erin could reply, Avery skipped off with Eva. It was a comfort to know Avery had made such a fast friend, and after yesterday's visit, Erin looked forward to becoming better friends with Christina.

On their way into the classroom, a fortysomething brunette came over to greet them. Christina introduced her as Gwen Ulbright, Pastor Terry's wife. "We're so happy to have you," Gwen said. "Help yourself to some coffee. We'll get started in a few minutes."

As Erin filled a cup, Diana Willoughby from the doughnut shop said hello. Pouring coffee for herself, she said, "I have to apologize again about that shelf. Did Kent have any trouble repairing it?"

"All fixed." The mention of Kent's name brought back the awkwardness of yesterday afternoon. Erin wasn't sure why she hadn't wanted to tell Avery about her first encounter with Kent…or maybe she knew exactly why. Protecting Avery was Erin's number one priority, and she didn't want her daughter to worry for a second that her mother might have put herself in a precarious situation.

Diana stirred a dollop of creamer into her coffee. "Kent's quiet, keeps to himself mostly, but you couldn't ask for a nicer guy—as a handyman or as a friend." She angled a meaningful smile toward Erin. "I've been hoping someone special would come into his life… especially someone who might entice him to come to church once in a while."

Diana's message came through loud and clear, and only reinforced Erin's reservations. If and when she ever allowed a new romantic interest into her life, he'd have to be a rock-solid believer.

Distracted by the new surroundings and her own rampant thoughts, Erin had a difficult time focusing on the lesson and was relieved when class ended. The worship service and familiar praise songs proved more settling…until the pastor's message on Jesus's parable about the three servants who were each given a certain number of talents to invest. Erin saw herself too clearly as the servant who buried his portion in the ground, with nothing to show for it when the owner returned. Was God unhappy with her because she'd long ago buried her own "talent" when she'd given up her plans to become an interior designer?

She'd latched onto basketry as an outlet for her creativity, only to endure Payne's punishment for wasting her time on a useless hobby when she should have been focusing on his needs and her duties as a homemaker. Not long afterward, she'd packed away her supplies and left them untouched until only a few months ago after moving in with Greg. The feel of rush, sea grass, reeds and twigs through her fingers, the sense of creating something beautiful from materials created by God set her free from the hurtful memories, temporarily at least, and carried her to a place of peace.

But now, with her job at the gift shop starting tomorrow, plus the excitement she'd felt at sharing her cabin redecorating ideas with the Austins, was this finally her chance to reclaim the dream she'd once set aside?

On their way out of church, Christina asked if she could take Erin up on her offer to go shopping together. "I know you're starting at Wanda's tomorrow. What are your hours?"

"I'll be working weekdays, nine to one. We could meet afterward and then shop until the kids get out of school."

"Perfect. Would tomorrow afternoon work for you?"

"I'll look forward to it."

Then on Monday morning, when Erin backed down the driveway to take Avery to school, she found the wooden post supporting her mailbox had splintered.

"Just call Mr. Ritter, Mommy," Avery said from the back seat. "He can fix it."

This was getting to be an uncomfortable habit. And

since when had Avery decided she didn't have to run interference between Erin and Kent?

Saturday, of course, when he'd wormed his way into the little girl's heart with an introduction to his horses.

Erin couldn't exactly do without a mailbox, so after dropping Avery at school, she had just enough time to stop at the hardware store before heading downtown. Finding Kent on duty, she didn't know whether to be thankful or disappear quickly and come back another time. He'd already seen her, though, and she browsed a few minutes while he finished arranging a display of paint supplies near the entrance. There was no denying how incredible he looked in faded jeans and a navy Zipp's Hardware polo shirt, his muscled arms tanned from working outdoors.

Striding over, he greeted her with a questioning smile. "That shelf didn't collapse on you again, I hope."

"No, your repairs are holding up fine." She blew out through pursed lips. "But now my mailbox post is broken."

Kent nodded. "Probably rotted off in the ground. I can fix it, no problem. Will you be home around noon?"

"I'm starting my new job today. I don't get off until one." Shifting her shoulder bag to the other arm, Erin bit back a discouraged groan. "I was supposed to meet a friend to go shopping afterward, but I guess we can reschedule."

"No need. I'll have it all done by the time you get home."

"Um, how much will it cost?"

"A plain wood post won't be more than twenty bucks."

Another expense Erin hadn't counted on, but not as bad as she'd feared. "And your labor?"

"On the house."

"Kent…you've got to stop doing this. I feel indebted enough already." Tears threatened. Erin blinked several times and glanced away.

In the next moment, she felt Kent's hand on her arm, and, though after years of living with Payne her instinct was to jerk free, she sensed no threat from this man. She willed a steadying breath into her lungs.

"It isn't about payback, Erin. It's about helping out a friend." He continued softly, almost as if to himself, "Everybody needs a little help from time to time."

"Even you?" she asked with a doubtful smirk. "The guy who apparently can fix anything?"

He glanced away, jaw tensing as he muttered, "Not everything."

Worried she'd brought up an unpleasant memory, she opened her mouth to apologize but decided instead to try a little humor. "Yes, I see it now. You're *not* so good at fixing your own lunch."

The light in his eyes returned as laughter burst from his throat. "You nailed me. If it doesn't come frozen, boxed or in a can, it isn't happening."

"Cooking can be fun, though. Ever thought of taking lessons?"

Kent wiggled his brows. "You offering?"

She quickly shook her head. "Even if I wanted to, my plate is full—excuse the pun. And," she said, checking her watch, "I need to be on my way before my new boss fires me on my very first day. Maybe you could say a few prayers…" Her words trailed into awkward silence.

With a tight smile, Kent replied, "Pretty sure God's

written me off, but I'll keep a good thought for you."
He started for the checkout counter. "Let me ring up
your mailbox post, and I'll head over to install it after
I finish my shift."

Hurrying to catch up, she fished her checkbook from
her purse. "Maybe you'll let me thank you by making
you a home-cooked dinner sometime?"

"Wouldn't turn it down."

As she wrote a check, she questioned her own judgment in allowing Kent into her life. Hadn't her mistake
marrying Payne taught her anything? He'd never even
pretended to be a believer, but she'd stupidly hoped she
could change him.

It was a mistake she couldn't afford to make again.

Approaching the front door of the gift shop a minute
before nine, Erin spotted a plump raven-haired woman
watching for her. "Hi, are you Wanda?"

"Wanda Flynn, at your service. And I'd know you
anywhere from your brother's description. Come on
in, Erin." Wanda's colorful maxi dress swayed as she
stepped aside. "We don't open until ten, but there's
plenty of prep work to do each morning. Today you
can fill out employment forms, and then I'll show you
around and explain your job duties."

With a nervous swallow, Erin hugged her purse to
her abdomen. "My brother did inform you I don't have
any retail sales experience?"

"Nothin' to it, honey. Besides, Greg said you always
wanted to be an interior decorator, so that's pretty much
what you'll be doing here, helping our customers choose
special items to enhance their spaces."

Wanda's Wonders definitely carried a plethora of

unique gifts and home decor. As Wanda took her on a tour of the various displays, she gazed in admiration and hoped she'd eventually earn enough to afford a few of the decorative pieces that caught her eye.

The tour ended with a lesson in operating the cash register, which sent waves of panic through Erin. When she flubbed a practice sales entry for the fourth time, she blew out an exasperated breath. "Sorry, I never was much good with computers."

"Mmm-hmm, I can see that." Wanda gave a solemn nod. "There are plenty of other things you can do around here, honey. Don't worry, we'll find your niche."

Grateful not to have gotten herself fired after only forty-five minutes on the job, Erin paid even closer attention to her other duties. Shadowing Wanda throughout the morning, she quickly picked up on reading customers' nonverbal cues as to whether they just wanted to browse or might welcome some assistance and advice. And while she might be all thumbs with the cash register, she found inventory management much easier to grasp.

When one o'clock rolled around, she was both exhausted and exhilarated. It felt good to be productive again, and even though she might still be a long way from an interior design career, sharing decorating tips as she helped customers find just what they were looking for brought its own kind of fulfillment. It made her even more excited about meeting with Christina to shop for the guest ranch cabins.

Then her cell phone rang as she strode out to her car. Christina's name appeared on the display.

"I hate to cancel at the last minute," she said, sounding frazzled, "but one of the twins is running a fever. Can we try again another day?"

"Of course. I hope your baby feels better soon." Saying goodbye, Erin tried to shake off her disappointment.

On the other hand, as stressful as the day had started out, she could use a couple of hours to kick back before picking up Avery at school. Besides, her stomach loudly informed her it was an hour past her usual lunchtime.

When she turned onto her street, she glimpsed a tan pickup parked in front of her house, and next to it, Kent had just attached her mailbox to a new white post. She'd almost forgotten he'd be coming by, and as she pulled into the driveway, her heart gave an unexpected lift.

"Hi," she called, stepping from her car. "How's it going?"

"Just finishing up."

"It looks great!" Erin stepped partway into the street for a better look. "Have you had lunch yet?"

"Uh, no. But I thought you had a shopping date."

"Christina's baby is sick."

Kent latched his toolbox and started toward his pickup. "Christina Austin, from Serenity Hills?"

"Yes, she asked if I'd give her some suggestions for redecorating their guest cabins."

He peered over his shoulder with a thoughtful frown. "You do that kind of thing? I mean, professionally?"

"No, not really." *Not yet anyway.* She heaved a shrug. "It's always been an interest of mine, and like you keep saying, it's just friends helping friends."

Setting his toolbox in the pickup, Kent gave a noncommittal grunt. It was obvious he had something on his mind.

Erin edged closer. "I was serious about lunch. Want to come in for a sandwich?"

Until a couple of days ago, one day in Kent's life was pretty much like the next. He thrived on the seasonal routines of cattle ranching combined with the structure of working at the hardware store. Even when the occasional problem arose, there was a level of predictability, exactly the way he liked it.

Then two things had happened. He'd learned the Juniper Bluff Historical Society wanted to include his tumbledown old house on the sesquicentennial tour, and Erin Dearborn had stepped into his life.

He wasn't sure which had him more shook-up.

He should have said no to the sandwich and headed on home. But his voice didn't cooperate, and the next thing he knew, he was sitting at Erin's elegantly set table. Again.

She brought over two plates. "I made ham sandwiches. Hope that's okay."

"Better 'n okay." He noted a few more pictures and artsy things decorating walls and surfaces. "Starting to look like home around here."

"I'd hoped to be further along before starting work today." Erin's shoulders rose and fell in a tired sigh. "Iced tea okay?"

"Fine. So how'd your first day go?"

"It was fun, actually—although I've been banned from ringing up purchases." A weak laugh escaped. "I do well to manage a personal email account and keep up with my brothers on Facebook. Anything requiring more computer literacy than that and I'm lost."

Admiring the artful lines of the fruit basket, Kent

shook his head. "You should ask Wanda to carry your baskets at the shop. Bet they'd sell fast."

"My baskets? Oh, no, that's just something I do for myself." Erin set the tea glasses on the table and took her seat. She paused and started to bow her head but then seemed to change her mind—no doubt on his account. After laying her napkin in her lap, she picked up her sandwich.

Annoyed with himself that he'd kept her from saying grace, he filled the silence with a question. "How'd you learn to make such pretty baskets?"

"A college course piqued my interest. Then a few years ago, I took a class at a community center, something to do for fun. For *me*." Her blue eyes turned smoky, and she glanced away. "My little hobby only made things worse, unfortunately."

Kent wondered what kind of man wouldn't want his wife doing something that made her so happy, something she had a genuine talent for—but he sensed Erin wasn't ready to share more details. And besides, how close did he really want to get to this woman?

A lot closer.

"So tell me more about yourself," Erin said, interrupting his thoughts. "It must be so rewarding to be able to fix things."

"Learned most of it from my dad. He's what you'd call a tinkerer. Always has a little project going in his garage workshop." Chewing a bite of sandwich, Kent suffered a moment of wistfulness. It had been too long since he and his dad had worked on a project together. But then, that was mostly Kent's fault for moving so far away. "Unfortunately, I haven't spent a lot of time fixing up my own house, as you probably noticed."

Erin offered a wry smile. "I did wonder about that."

With a rough cough, he decided to brave the subject he'd been avoiding ever since the letter from the historical society had arrived. "Look, I know you're busy with your daughter and the new job and all, but I'm kind of up a creek about a situation I recently found out about."

She shot him an uneasy glance. "What kind of situation, exactly?"

"Seems my house might qualify as a local historical site." He explained about the Juniper Bluff sesquicentennial celebration. "If I agree to let them put it on the tour, I'm gonna have to do a lot of sprucing up. I'm good with repairs and painting and such, but the inside stuff? Wouldn't know where to begin."

"Oh. Are you asking for my help?"

"Yeah, I guess I am. But we've got plenty of time. The big event is more than a year away."

Erin pushed her empty plate aside and fingered her napkin. "I've never even contemplated redoing a historical home. Wouldn't there be certain requirements about recreating the original appearance?"

"Got me. I'll try to find out. In the meantime, would you at least think about it? And I fully intend to pay you for your expertise," he added quickly.

She shook her head firmly. "I couldn't accept money. Not after how you've traded repairs at my house for nothing more than lunch." Her smile brightened. "Besides, weren't we just talking about friends helping friends?"

"That we were." Kent pushed away from the table. "And lunch was great—thanks again."

"And thank *you* for coming to my rescue again."

Erin walked him out to his pickup. "Diana Willoughby was right."

His brows shot up. "Is Diana spreading rumors about me?"

"She just said you're a really nice guy to have as a handyman…" Cheeks reddening, Erin glanced away. "And as a friend."

An unexpected burst of elation swelled beneath Kent's breastbone. He climbed in behind the wheel, and with the door still open, he started the engine. "Anytime you need a hand around here, all you have to do is ask." He chuckled. "Especially if there's a meal involved."

She smiled and stepped closer. "I mean it, thank you."

Tipping his hat, he pulled the door closed. Had he really just suggested spending even more time with this woman? Man, he must be losing it. Because if any woman had half a chance of luring him out of his bachelor ways, it was Erin Dearborn.

Chapter Five

Three afternoons later, Kent rode out to check on his pregnant cows. Disappointment struck again—no chance he'd have nearly enough calves to take to market next fall to make it worth his while. All the more reason he needed to buy the bull he'd had his eye on and build up his herd.

Afterward, as he released Jasmine into her pasture, his cell phone rang. By now, he had Erin's name and number in his contacts. Seeing the call was from her, he got a little hitch in his breath.

"Erin. What's up?"

"Hi, Kent." She hesitated. "Am I interrupting anything important?"

He sensed the *I'm sorry* lingering at the edges of her question. Striving for a light tone, he answered, "No problem. Just taking care of some ranch chores. Wait—do *you* have a problem?"

"Actually, yes. Who knew an older home would have so many issues?"

"Hey, try living in a hundred-and-fifty-year-old farmhouse."

Her laughter warmed him through and through. "Then I guess you might know something about leaky pipes. When I got home from picking up Avery from school, we found water coming out from under the refrigerator."

"Sounds like the ice-maker connection." Already making a mental list of items to pick up at the hardware store, he headed toward his truck. "I can be there in half an hour."

"Thank you." Relief flooded Erin's tone. "And for zis evening's menu," she added with a fake French accent, "ze chef is preparing an exquisite chicken casserole."

Kent belted out a laugh. "Did I say half an hour? Let's make it twenty minutes."

The repair turned out to be exactly what he'd predicted—replacing an older pipe fitting and shutoff valve. He dreaded the moment he finished, knowing it meant more haggling with Erin about paying him.

"I'm telling you," he said as he cleaned up behind the refrigerator, "if that chicken casserole tastes as good as it smells, that's all I need."

She took the wet paper towels he handed her. "But the parts weren't free. You have to tell me how much."

"Okay, okay." With the fridge back in place, Kent added up what he'd paid for the parts, which reflected his employee discount, and Erin wrote him a check.

He washed up while Erin got supper on the table, then suffered a different kind of awkwardness when Avery asked if they could sing her favorite table blessing.

Erin cast a quick glance at Kent. "Maybe we should just pray silently this time, honey."

"No, please, go ahead," he said with an uneasy smile. "I'd love to hear y'all sing."

"You have to sing with us," Avery insisted. "It's a round. I start, then Mommy starts, then you start. And then you finish last."

Before either he or Erin could protest, Avery burst out with the opening lines. "God our Father, God our Father..."

With a resigned shrug, Erin chimed in with her soft soprano, and when it was Kent's turn, Avery tapped his arm. He choked out a husky "God our Father" and mumbled what he could remember of the rest of the verse but faded out as Erin sang her last lilting amens.

"That's okay." Avery gave a condescending nod. "Next time, you'll know all the words."

Next time? How many more reminders did Kent need that he was on the outs with God? Even his parents didn't put this much pressure on him—maybe because they lived more than five hundred miles away and he didn't see them that often.

Through the rest of the meal, Avery chattered on about her school day and getting to help her teacher clean out the gerbil cage again. Kent didn't get a chance to ask how Erin's first week at work was going until Avery ran off to play after supper ended.

"I'm enjoying it," Erin said as she set a dish of leftovers in the fridge. "When Greg told me I'd be working at a gift shop, I never realized my interior design education would turn out to be such an asset. But already, several customers have asked me for decorating advice before deciding on a purchase."

"Good, you'll be getting plenty of practice before I need you to start on my place." Kent gathered up his hat and toolbox.

"Have you found out anything more from the historical society?"

"Went by after work yesterday to apply for official designation and got a copy of the guidelines. A lot of mumbo jumbo I need to wade through."

Erin followed him through the den. "When you figure it out, let me know how I can help."

"Appreciate it."

On his way out, he happened to glance through an open door into what appeared to be Erin's workroom. A large half-finished basket, more than a foot across, sat on a folding table amid several thin twigs and long strips of some kind of grass. Kent did a quick change of direction and strode into the room.

"Couldn't resist a closer look," he said as Erin stepped up beside him. "What's your plan for this one?"

"Not sure yet. I just started on it a couple of days ago." She picked up a twig and began working it through the basket ribs.

Following the deft movements of her fingers, Kent wished he had all day to watch. "Will you show me the finished product when you're done?"

She looked up at him, her expression thoughtful. "I'll do even better. It'll be my thank-you gift for all the help you've given me."

Kent gave a low whistle. "Wow. It'll sure catch everyone's eye when they come out for the sesquicentennial tour."

Her smile in response skewered straight through his heart.

On his way home from the hardware store on Friday, Kent stopped at the mailbox before turning up the driveway, and the sight of his own tilted, weathered post evoked fresh thoughts of Erin.

As he stepped from the pickup, the blast of a horn jolted him like an explosion, and for a paralyzing moment, he was back in Afghanistan. Would he ever completely get past the PTSD he'd battled off and on since leaving the service? After several steadying breaths and an apologetic wave to LeRoy, his crusty neighbor, he grabbed his mail, then jumped back in the truck and pulled into the driveway.

When he stepped through the screen porch into the kitchen, Skip met him with a wagging tail. The old dog might be lazy and shed like crazy, but he truly was a comfort.

"Decided to get up off the couch, huh?" Kent scratched the dog's head with one hand and flipped through the mail with the other. He tossed a couple of bills onto the stack he planned to work on this weekend and dropped the advertising fliers into the plastic recycling tub on the porch.

One piece of mail caught his eye, the Nebraska return address as unfamiliar as the sender's handwriting. Even more confusing, the letter hadn't been directed to Kent personally but to *Owner* at Kent's address.

Plopping down in a kitchen chair, he pried open the flap and pulled out a folded sheet of cream-colored stationery. The same looping handwriting filled the page, and tucked inside was an old-style color photograph. A haunting sense of familiarity gave him pause as he studied the picture of a stately white farmhouse. Neatly trimmed shrubbery and beds of flowers in full bloom surrounded the house. A wide expanse of green lawn filled the foreground.

Then it dawned on him. This was *his* house!

Stunned, he turned his attention to the letter.

To whom it may concern, it began, and went on to explain that the sender's elderly father, Nelson Gilliam, had grown up in Kent's house. The man now suffered from heart failure, and as his condition worsened, he reminisced more and more about his boyhood days on the ranch.

The writer continued:

I recently heard about the Juniper Bluff sesquicentennial planned for next year, but the doctors have serious doubts my father can survive that long. It would mean so much to him if he could see the old place one more time. Could we prevail upon you to permit us to visit, possibly early this summer?

The letter was signed by Mr. Gilliam's daughter, Jean Thompson, and included her phone number and email address.

Kent laid the letter on the table, then briskly rubbed his eyes. Much as he'd like to honor her request, how could he? The way things looked now, the old guy probably wouldn't even recognize the place—or if he did, it might distress him even more. Thoughts roaming beyond the walls, Kent pictured the unkempt shrubs, the flower beds he'd surrendered to weeds, the lawn sparse and brown. The house itself desperately needed painting, and the porch steps could easily swallow a man whole if he didn't tread carefully.

And if the outside looked so beautifully kept in Jean Thompson's photo, Kent could only imagine the care her grandparents had given the inside.

Besides, summer was only a couple of months away, and Kent had been counting on at least a year to spruce up the place, not to mention getting his head around having a bunch of strangers wandering around. If it weren't for the tax-reduction incentive and how badly he needed that bull, he wouldn't have been considering the historical designation at all.

Heaving a groan, he shifted to the other end of the table, where his laptop computer was buried beneath ads from last Sunday's paper, his cattle tally book, the documents from the historical society and the cereal bowl that never quite made it to the sink that morning. After shoving everything aside, he opened the computer and clicked the icon for his email program. He copied Jean Thompson's address into the to line and then gnawed the inside of his lip while he figured out a sensitive way to decline.

Dear Mrs. Thompson, he began.

I received your letter today, and I'm very sorry about your father's condition. But I'm afraid the house isn't the showplace it used to be—

Scratch that. Did he really want it to sound like he'd totally neglected everything? Even if he had?

But a lot of time has passed, and I'm afraid things won't look quite like your father remembers them.

Better.

So I would hate for you to bring him on such a long and tiring trip only to be disappointed. I appreciate seeing the picture of how things used to look, though. Please let me know if you'd like it returned.

Nodding with satisfaction, Kent typed his name and hit Send.

He sat back and stretched out one leg, only to find Skip staring up at him, one eye narrowed as if the old dog were judging him for his cowardice.

"Don't look at me that way." Kent shook a finger at the dog. "I can't be this guy's hero and make his last days better."

Truth was, he was no kind of hero at all. Just a cowboy doing everything in his power to live a peaceful, uneventful life.

The following Sunday morning, Palm Sunday, Erin laughed with Christina as their daughters marched out after the worship service, waving their palm branches and singing "Hosanna in the highest!" at the top of their lungs.

"That'll probably go on all day," Christina said, pushing the twins in their stroller. "And I'm so glad Eva has made such a good friend." She'd told Erin how timid Eva and her brother Joseph had been when Christina first came to Serenity Hills.

"I'm glad to have made a friend, too." Erin offered a warm smile. "And we still need to reschedule that shopping trip."

Christina drew Erin into a quick hug. "Maybe one day this week? After the Camp Serenity kids leave this afternoon, I'll be more than ready for some retail therapy."

"Sure. Give me a call." Erin said goodbye and walked with Avery over to their sedan.

"I wish I could do the camp," Avery said as she climbed into her booster seat. "I bet they're having so much fun."

Buckling in behind the wheel, Erin caught Avery's eye in the rearview mirror and beamed a sympathetic smile. "I'm sure they are, honey. But you know the camp is for kids who don't have all the nice things you do."

"But aren't we poor now, too? You always say we can't buy stuff because you don't have any money."

Leave it to a seven-year-old. Erin turned out of the parking lot to head home. "It's still not the same, Avery. Many of the campers have difficult lives at home. Or they may not even have a real family—a mom and dad who are able to care for them like they should."

Avery lowered her voice to barely above a whisper. "Well, I don't have a daddy anymore, either."

Regret tightened like steel bands around Erin's chest as she prayed for the best way to respond. No matter how badly Payne had hurt her, both physically and emotionally, she'd tried her best not to speak badly of him to their daughter. "You *do* have a daddy," she said with as much assurance as she could muster. "Even though we don't live with him any longer, he's still your dad, and I know he loves you very much." As much as her self-centered ex-husband could love anyone.

Avery spent a few moments in silence as Erin drove through town. As they turned up their street, she said, "Eva's daddy is nice, so all daddies prob'ly aren't mean."

"No, honey." Erin could hardly force the words past her aching throat. "Most daddies are very, very nice."

Arriving home gave Erin the chance to change the subject as she reheated the leftover chicken casserole from Thursday's supper with Kent. Recalling his lame attempt to sing along with their table prayer, she smiled.

Even if he'd only tried for Avery's sake, there was a man who'd know how to be a good father.

The instant the thought formed, Erin banished it. She was nowhere near ready for anything resembling a relationship—with Kent, or any other man on the planet. Least of all with someone so resistant toward God.

Later, while waiting for her brother to come by after finishing up with the Camp Serenity kids, she worked on the basket she'd decided to give to Kent. Hearing the doorbell, she hurried to the entryway in time to see Avery wrapping her uncle in a big hug.

Greg grinned at Erin over the little girl's head. "Apparently, I'm not the only one arriving on your doorstep this afternoon." He tipped his head toward the driveway, where Erin glimpsed a familiar tan pickup. "This guy says he's your handyman?"

"Yes, he's been doing some repairs around the house." Erin peered around her brother to see Kent hefting a large cardboard box from the back of his truck. "What in the world—"

Arms full, Kent greeted Erin with a nod as he ambled up the walk. "Guess I should have called first." He acknowledged Greg with a hesitant smile. "Didn't mean to intrude."

"That's okay," Greg replied. One eyebrow raised, he cast Erin a meaningful glance. And, boy, did she catch his meaning. Greg opened the door wider for Kent. "Need any help?"

"Got it just fine." Kent eased past Greg. To Erin, he said, "Mind if I take this straight to your workroom?"

She looked at him askance. "First, maybe you should tell me what's in the box."

"Just some interesting stuff I've collected while riding through the pasture. Thought you might use some of it for your baskets."

"Really? Thank you." Heart fluttering, she showed Kent into the workroom, where he set the box on the floor next to her table. She peeked inside to find a variety of grasses, plant stems and pliable twigs. "This is wonderful! How did you know I was running low on supplies?"

"Didn't really. Just saving you another adventure in the wilds of the Hill Country," he added with a wink. With a hesitant glance at Greg, he tipped his hat and shuffled toward the door. "Best be on my way. Y'all have a nice visit."

"Don't rush off on my account." Greg still hadn't wiped the mischievous grin off his face. With an arch look at Erin, he said, "Yes, do tell me more about your *adventures*, little sis."

"It was nothing. I accidentally ended up on Kent's property the other day while searching for some basketry materials."

"It was for my birthday basket," Avery chimed in. "And Mommy just told me yesterday that she even got to ride Mr. Ritter's horse that day."

"Is that so?" Greg turned to Kent and thrust out his hand. "Then let me congratulate you for accomplishing a feat no one else has been able to achieve."

Erin winced. "My brother and niece have been trying to get me to ride for years, but I've been too scared."

"I thought you did just fine." Kent's gaze softened into a look that made Erin's pulse quicken.

Never in all the years she'd been married to Payne had he ever looked at her quite that way. Never with such tender understanding. Never with such quiet admiration.

"Well—" Kent dipped his chin "—I should go."

"I'll walk you out." Following him, Erin shot her brother a sharp warning glance.

Kent paused on the porch, his lips parting as if he wanted to say something. Then his jaw clamped shut, and with a brisk nod, he settled his hat deeper on his head. "Be seein' ya."

"Thank you again for the supplies. I still can't believe you did that."

"Just bein' neighborly." Lips askew, he sidled toward the front walk. Clearly, something else was on his mind.

Thinking quickly, Erin said, "I'll probably finish your basket by tomorrow. Maybe I could bring it by your place before I pick up Avery from school?"

"No need to make a special trip."

Erin cast him a dubious frown. "Isn't that what you did for me this afternoon?"

"I was coming to town anyway. For groceries and… stuff."

Why didn't she completely believe him? "Well, I might be driving out in the country after work tomorrow for…*stuff*." She punctuated the word with a wiggle of her brows. "So if I happen to drop by with your basket, would that be okay?"

Looking toward the street, Kent scratched the back of his neck. "Yeah." When he stepped off the porch, they were at eye level, and he met her smile with a shy one of his own. "I'll be sure to stay close to the house."

"Great. See you then."

Kent drove away wondering what had possessed him today. Lately, he'd been doing and thinking things so completely out of character that if it weren't so disconcerting, it would have been hilarious. Seriously, Kent Ritter, the man without an aesthetic bone in his body, scouting for pretty grasses and plant parts to present as a gift to a woman he barely knew?

Well, he did have an ulterior motive. Not long after he'd emailed his response to Jean Thompson, she'd replied with another plea for his indulgence.

I sincerely hope you'll reconsider, her message began.

My dad hasn't much left besides his memories. I wish you could see how his face lights up when he's reminiscing about growing up on the ranch or telling stories from his navy days. I've even tried contacting one or two of his navy buddies, but those he was closest with have already passed away.

The mention of Nelson Gilliam's naval service had struck a nerve with Kent, and now he was second-guessing his refusal. How could he deny a fellow veteran what little happiness seeing his childhood home might bring? But no way could he crush the man's memories by letting him see the house and grounds looking so neglected. If he was going to change his mind about letting Mrs. Thompson and her father visit this summer, he'd have to drastically accelerate his timetable for sprucing things up.

He'd been all set to share the change of plans with Erin when he'd dropped by, but her brother had just gotten there, and Kent felt awkward about intruding—especially when he caught the matchmaking glint in Greg O'Grady's eyes. Kent had seen that look so many times before on the faces of his Juniper Bluff acquaintances. Somebody always had a sister or friend or niece or granddaughter Kent ought to meet. Or if he offered the least bit of polite attention to an attractive single woman, people were ready to start planning his engagement party.

It was getting downright embarrassing.

Home from his shift at the hardware store on Monday, he grabbed a bite for lunch and did a quick check on the herd, then berated himself for pacing between the house and barn while watching the road for a glimpse of Erin's car. Even lazy old Skip had picked up on Kent's agitation. The dog trailed his steps and whined as if anticipating something momentous—which, in Skip's narrow world, usually involved extra treats or a truck ride to see the vet.

Shortly before two, Erin's car rolled up the driveway. Kent had just finished washing out the horses' water pails and feed pans, and with all the splotches on his T-shirt and jeans, he wished he'd had a chance to clean up before she arrived. Oh, well, too late.

He reached her car as she lifted the finished basket from the back seat. "Ah, man," he said, whistling out a breath. "That is amazing."

"Do you really like it?" She smiled up at him, the need for approval shimmering in her blue eyes.

"Are you kidding?" Kent took the basket from her and turned it in every direction so he could admire the intricacies of Erin's handiwork. When Skip stretched up to sniff the basket, Kent moved it out of reach. "No, fella. This is definitely not a dog toy."

"This is your dog?" Erin was already giving Skip a good scratch behind the ears.

"Erin, meet Skip, the laziest, most good-for-nothing animal on the planet."

She glanced up with a disbelieving frown, then returned her attention to the dog. "Hey, boy, aren't you a sweetheart!"

Kent chuckled. So horses scared Erin, but big, hairy, slobbery dogs obviously didn't. Remembering what he wanted to talk to her about, he cleared his throat. "Can you stay for a bit? I'd like to talk more about fixing up my house."

Her gaze turned serious as she straightened. "Did you figure out the historical designation requirements?"

"Working on it. But something else has come up." Shifting the basket to brace it against his hip, he described Jean Thompson's request and their follow-up emails. "I'd like to do this for the old guy, but you see what the place looks like." He swept his hand toward the barn, the house, the yard, then shrugged in frustration.

Erin cast him a sympathetic smile. "Why do I get the feeling the inside of your house looks just as neglected as everything else?"

"Because it'd be true." Kent winced. "I can do the painting and repairs—I've certainly put it off long enough—but making everything look nice, like a real home where a family could live…"

His voice trailed off at the thought that his house might one day be a *home* again. That someday, perhaps, he might even have a family of his own. Giving a snort, he adjusted his hat. "Anyway, I wanted to show you the picture Mrs. Thompson sent so you could see how everything used to look back when her dad lived here."

"Yes, I'd love to see the photo—and the rest of your house, too." Erin's eyes sparkled with anticipation. "If I'm going to be your decorator, I'd better know what I'm up against."

Chapter Six

Stepping through Kent's back door, Erin swallowed a gasp. Yes, a bachelor definitely lived here. Random stacks of mail and newspapers covered half the oblong kitchen table. At the far end, a laptop computer peeked out from beneath even more papers. The only item adorning the drab walls was a Zipp's Hardware calendar open to April. The photo of the month showed a guy in a baseball cap waving from the seat of a shiny new riding lawn mower.

An empty coffee mug sat next to what looked to be Kent's to-do list. Scooting past her, Kent made a space on the table for the basket. He snatched up the mug and rinsed it in the sink, then turned to Erin with a nervous grin. "As you can see, I'm not exactly prepared for company."

Smiling, she ran a finger along the windowsill. Hardly a trace of dust. Except for the clutter, Kent appeared to keep things fairly clean, even if he didn't spend much time on the niceties. "How long since you've done anything to the house?"

"You mean besides move in?"

Erin cast him a knowing wink. "Let's see the photo."

Riffling through some papers, Kent found the picture and held it out to her. "You'd hardly know it was the same place."

Hand to her chest, Erin breathed out a sigh. "It's beautiful. It's…"

"Impossible?" Hopelessness tinged Kent's tone. "Be honest with me. Because I can email Mrs. Thompson right back and say this visit can't happen."

"No. Don't." Emotion tightened Erin's throat. How could she ever explain how the house in this picture so perfectly matched the pristine white Victorian home she once dreamed might be her own someday? The graceful porches and dormer windows. Myriad flowers adding color and greenery. A strong, tall tree with a rope swing, and a grassy lawn where children could play. "We can do this, Kent. If we get started right away, we can make this happen."

They sat down together at the table to study the information provided by the county's historical preservation commission. While Kent wasn't required to replicate the original late-nineteenth-century decor, there were stipulations about communicating a sense of the past, even with twenty-first-century modernizations. An inspection would be performed prior to final certification.

With those criteria in mind, Erin's excitement about the project grew. She asked for a paper and a pen and jotted notes as they walked from room to room. Afterward, they made a circuit around the exterior and noted any needed repairs. A fresh coat of paint, inside and out, became a top priority. Erin could already envision color schemes—a cheery yellow for the kitchen, cocoa beige for the living room, pastel blues, greens and mauves for the bedrooms. Coordinating window coverings and furniture accents would add an extra touch of country charm.

Before leaving to pick up Avery from school, Erin provided Kent with a list of tasks to get started on, beginning with scraping and prepping the exterior for painting. "We need to choose the perfect shade of charcoal gray for the shutters and trim to set off the white siding. I'll come by the hardware store before work tomorrow to look at paint color samples."

Kent walked her to her car. "With Avery and your real job, are you sure you have the time to spare?"

"Are you kidding? Redecorating an entire house like this is a dream come true. It's going to be fun." The most fun she'd had in a long time. Climbing in behind the wheel, she beamed a smile. "I'll see you in the morning."

But when she glimpsed Kent in the rearview mirror, it wasn't enthusiasm she saw in his expression. It was more like, *What have I gotten myself into?*

Had she been overly enthusiastic? It was Kent's house after all. Uncertainty carved a hole in the pit of her stomach, a feeling she'd grown far too familiar with during her marriage to Payne. Always second-guessing herself, she could never be sure whether the next thing she said or did would flip his mood like a light switch, sending him into morose self-pity or all-out rage. Everything—*everything*—about her life with Payne had been about keeping him happy and on an even keel. And all too often she'd failed.

Behold, I make all things new, God said. Which meant Erin had to stop dwelling on the past. And she had to stop projecting her experience with Payne onto good men like Kent—exactly as she'd tried to help Avery understand.

* * *

The next morning, after dropping Avery at school, Erin stopped by Diana's Donuts before driving over to the hardware store.

"Coffee and apple fritters for two, coming up," Diana said with a smirk as she filled Erin's order. "Sharing with anyone special?"

Erin slid some bills across the counter. "The extra is for Kent. I'm helping him with a project—that's all."

"Sorry, I shouldn't tease you." With an understanding smile, Diana handed Erin her change. "I know exactly how it feels to be the focus of the entire town's matchmaking attempts."

"Believe me, I'm far from ready to get involved with anyone. Right now, I'm all about taking care of my daughter and trying to move on with my life." Erin tucked a few extra napkins into the cardboard tray holding her coffees and said goodbye.

A few minutes later, she parked in front of Zipp's Hardware. Balancing the coffee tray in one hand and tucking her planning notebook under her other arm, she used her hip to nudge open the entrance door.

Expecting to find Kent in his usual spot up front, she was surprised to see an older man with sparse gray hair and a bushy mustache.

Barely glancing up from some kind of catalog spread open on the counter, the man offered a brusque "He'p ya, ma'am?"

She edged close enough to read the man's name tag: Ben Zipp. Must be the store owner. "I was looking for Kent."

"In the back." He tipped his head in the general direction.

She took the gesture as permission to find her own way and started down the nearest aisle. Approaching a short hallway leading to some offices, she heard voices, one of them definitely Kent's.

"You need to think long and hard about this, Elijah," Kent was saying. "Enlistment isn't something you want to rush into."

"I have thought about it, and college doesn't make sense for me. I can get what education I need in the service." The speaker's Texas twang gave a determined lilt to his tone. "Anyway, I want to serve my country."

"You really want to take a chance you'll face combat?" Kent's voice again, laced with plaintive intensity. "That you might see your best buddies dead on the battlefield?"

"I get that. I'm ready."

Several moments of silence followed. Then, "Son, you will *never* be ready."

The vehemence behind Kent's words made Erin tremble and turn away. The coffee tray tipped, and she sucked in a noisy breath. As she steadied the tray, boots clomped down the hall.

"Erin?"

She spun around, this time losing her notebook. The coffee tray would have hit the floor, too, if Kent hadn't grabbed it. "I'm so sorry. I didn't mean to eavesdrop—"

"It's okay." Even with the tension lines etching the corners of his mouth, he spoke calmly, seeming more concerned about her than whatever was going on in the office. "Why don't you wait for me over in the paint department? Aisle three. There's a counter and bar stools where we can sit and look at samples."

"If this is a bad time, we can do this another day."

Kent gently placed the coffee tray back in her hands, then stooped to retrieve her notebook. "It's okay, I said. I'll be there in a sec."

Erin found the counter midway along aisle three and shakily set down the cardboard tray. Sliding onto a bar stool, she mentally replayed the discussion she'd overheard. The Austins had mentioned he'd served in the military, and his harshness in replying to the young man suggested his battlefield experiences had left scars—if not physically, then most certainly emotionally. Could those experiences explain why he'd turned his back on God?

She could certainly identify with such wounds of the spirit, but at least she still had her faith. *Father,* she prayed, hands folded and head bent, *please heal Kent from his past, just as I've asked You to heal me. Help us both to live in full assurance of Your eternal love and—*

Footsteps approaching interrupted her prayer. She looked up as Kent drew near, a sadly curious frown skewing his lips. He scooted onto the stool beside her and softly cleared his throat. "Caught you praying for me, didn't I?"

She handed him a coffee and hoped it had stayed hot. "How did you know?"

"Because that's who you are." He took a tentative sip. "How do you do it anyway?"

"Do what—pray?" She tore open the pastry bag and set each of the glazed fritters on a napkin. "I can't *not* pray. As weak and helpless as I feel sometimes, leaning on God is all I can do to keep going."

Biting into his fritter, Kent seemed to chew on her words as much as he did the pastry, but he said nothing more on the subject, and Erin wouldn't pressure him. She'd have to trust God to bring Kent around in His own good time.

After a few minutes savoring their coffee and fritters, Kent suggested they take a look at some paint colors. Joining him in front of a display of exterior color samples, Erin selected several cards with shades ranging from pearly gray to the deepest charcoal.

"You shouldn't go too light or too dark," she said, and zeroed in on a color labeled Stormy Night. "What do you think of this one?"

"The blue undertones brighten it up." He held the sample against a white surface. "Nice contrast. I like it."

Erin chuckled. "Look at you getting all artsy."

"I know how to appreciate beauty." He looked straight at her, his deep brown eyes smoldering into their own interesting shade of gray.

Pulse skittering, Erin moved farther along the display. "Should we look at interior colors now?"

Just a friend helping a friend, she chided herself. This was not the time to let things get complicated.

Don't complicate things. Kent drew a slow, silent breath as Erin chose an assortment of interior paint color cards. Yeah, he was fighting a major attraction toward her, but that little scene with Elijah, the store's nineteen-year-old stock boy, was an unwelcome reminder that he still had issues to work through. Bad enough he could barely keep it together while advising an eager kid bent on serving his country. Add the fact that he and Erin remained so far apart in their faith lives, and he saw little hope for anything between them beyond friendship.

Except…he couldn't shake the feeling that Erin and

her daughter had come into his life for a reason. And if there was a reason, then there had to be a Someone to whom that reason belonged. And if there was a Someone, it meant God might actually care about Kent Ritter.

He wasn't sure how he felt about that, but for the first time in a long time, it sparked hope.

Erin tapped the stack of color samples. "This should be enough for starters. I need to get to the gift shop, but can I get back to you with more ideas in a few days?"

"Sounds good. I'll start on the exterior prep this afternoon." Walking Erin to the front, Kent considered asking Elijah if he'd be interested in putting in a few hours with him to earn a little extra money. Might be a way to smooth things over—so long as Kent scaled back the whole forget-the-service-and-stay-in-school vibe.

At the exit, Erin paused. "Kent, I really appreciate being asked to help you with this project. It means a lot." A tentative smile teased the corners of her mouth. "More than you know."

Her expression alone told him how much it meant, and if he ever met up with the creep of an ex-husband who'd so badly damaged her self-confidence, the guy had better run the other way.

He thanked her for the coffee and fritter, then watched with a peculiar ache in his belly as she got in her car and drove out of the parking lot.

When he stepped back inside, Ben Zipp eyed him from beneath bushy white brows. "Who's the pretty lady?"

"Just a new friend. She's helping me with ideas for fixing up my house."

"'Bout time. And I'm *not* talking about fixing up your house," Ben harrumphed. "Although I'm sad to say it's about time for that, too. How long you been livin' in that run-down old shack anyway?"

"Long enough to know I don't need you butting into my business." Good thing Kent knew his boss well enough not to worry about getting fired for such a remark. Gruff as Ben Zipp might come across, he had a Texas-size heart matched by a wry sense of humor.

Ben came from behind the checkout counter to straighten a rack of do-it-yourself pamphlets. "You sure seem set on buttin' into Elijah's business about joining the service."

"That's different. He's a kid with no idea what he'd be getting himself into."

Ben skewered Kent with a one-eyed glare. "If somebody'd said the same to you back when you were ready to enlist, would you have listened?"

"No," he murmured, dropping his chin. "Fact is, my dad tried his best to talk me out of joining the navy. He hoped I'd take an interest in working at his auto dealership. But I thought I knew what I wanted, and it wasn't selling cars."

"So are you saying now you regret your choice? In hindsight, would you have done anything differently?"

Kent closed his eyes briefly. "Probably not."

"And are you proud of your service to your country?"

"Of course I am." Knowing he'd never win this argument, Kent heaved a resigned sigh. "I just hate the thought of another kid coming home from war with memories like the ones I live with day and night." He looked away, his voice fading. "Or not coming home at all."

"Well, that's not up to you, is it?" Ben sank a hand deep onto Kent's shoulder. "The good book says there's a time for everything. A time to be born, a time to die. A time for war, a time for peace. But it's all in God's hands, and He is trustworthy."

Before Kent could frame a polite response, which at the moment seemed beyond his capabilities, Elijah strode over. "Sorry to interrupt." The boy looked uneasily between Kent and Ben. "What did you want me to do with that shipment of garden tools?"

"Be right with you," Ben said, then turned to Kent. "Elijah and I've got the store covered this morning. Seems like you've got plenty of your own stuff to tend to."

Mouth firm, Kent nodded. He was pretty sure Ben wasn't referring to only the home-improvement project. More likely a *Kent*-improvement project. That, unfortunately, would require quite a bit more than a morning off.

After another trip down the paint aisle to select a few supplies, Kent rang up his own purchases and then headed out to his truck. Figuring he'd be using a whole different set of muscles on this paint job, he decided to stop at the drugstore on his way through town and pick up a supersize bottle of ibuprofen.

Purchase in hand, he started back to his truck, only to stop short beneath the purple awning over Wanda's Wonders. The window display showcased a variety of gift items and home decor, including custom-designed jewelry, handmade soaps and lotions, artsy wooden signs, frilly lampshades, decorative wreaths and artificial flower arrangements.

Kent didn't have to wonder why he'd never noticed the shop before. How many times had he ever been in the market for fancy soaps or cute signs? He also didn't need to ask why the store suddenly blipped loud and clear on his mental radar. This was the shop where Erin worked, and the mere thought of catching a glimpse of her sent his heart racing.

Hesitating for only a moment, he pushed open the shop door. A chime sounded as he entered, and a large woman with a bun piled high atop her head came forward to greet him.

"Howdy, and welcome to Wanda's Wonders!" A flowery, flowing skirt skimmed the woman's sandals. "Looking for something special for a special someone?"

"Actually, I, uh… I mean, a friend of mine works here, and I wanted to, uh…"

Erin stepped out from behind a curtain near the back. "Kent? Aren't you supposed to be at work?"

He waved shyly. "Ben gave me the day off to get started on the house." *Among other reasons.* "Passed your shop and thought I'd stop in."

"Oh. Would you like to look around? We carry all sorts of decorative items for the home, and you might find something—"

"Honey," Wanda interrupted with a knowing smirk, "I strongly suspect this handsome fella has something besides shopping in mind."

A blush to match her fiery-red hair crept up her cheeks, and Kent hoped his arrival wasn't getting Erin in trouble with her boss. He glanced around at the myriad gifts and handcrafted items displayed throughout the crowded shop. "Maybe another time," he said. "That pretty basket you made for me will do just fine for now."

Wanda looked up with interest. "Erin, are you a basket maker?"

"It's just a hobby." With a self-conscious smile, she

turned away to shift a ceramic vase a fraction to the right.

Kent shook his head. "She's being modest. I've seen some of her stuff, and it's good. She's real creative with the designs, too."

Wanda pinned her thoughtful gaze on Erin. "Bring me some samples when you come in tomorrow. If they're as good as this young man says, I'll consider a consignment deal with you."

Kent couldn't tell from Erin's tight-lipped smile whether she was grateful for the opportunity or annoyed with him for butting in. Maybe both? A customer's arrival meant he'd have to wait for his answer. He just hoped his interference wouldn't cost him his interior decorator.

Chapter Seven

Ten minutes after Erin got home from work, Kent showed up at her front door. "I thought you went home to start painting."

"I did, but..." Hat held in front of his chest, he cast her a boyish smile. "I had to make sure you weren't mad at me."

"I should be. That's all Wanda could talk about after you left." She crossed her arms. "I told you, my baskets are like therapy. I've never seriously considered selling them."

"But it doesn't mean you couldn't." His expression pleading, Kent grasped one of her elbows. When she flinched, he immediately let go, then continued more gently, "You could use the money toward starting your own interior design business. You said that's what you'd studied for in college."

His logic made a crazy kind of sense—but even so, was she anywhere near ready to venture into business for herself? Fingers to her temple, she swiveled away. "I need to think about this."

"I get it. No pressure." Kent sidled toward the entryway. "So I'm gonna head back home and—"

"Would you help me pick out some baskets?"

He turned with a surprised smile. "To show Wanda? Be glad to."

Before she could talk herself out of it, she hurried to her workroom closet and brought out a large cardboard box containing some of her earlier basket creations. Strewing them across the worktable, she scrutinized each one.

Kent picked up a midsize sea grass basket with matching lid, only to set it down and snatch up two smaller baskets made from reeds. "There must be a dozen or more here. And you've had these sitting in your closet all this time? That's a crime, Erin. Someone could have been enjoying them."

His words stabbed her heart as she recalled Pastor Terry's message two Sundays ago about the servant who'd buried his talent in the ground. Though she sometimes gave her baskets as gifts, these she'd hoarded like private treasures, not unlike the rich man in another of Jesus's parables who took selfish pride in building bigger barns in which to store his grain. Had basketry become more of an avoidance method than the therapy she claimed it was? And if so, what did that *really* say about her faith?

Hands trembling, she sniffed back a tear and began packing all the baskets in the box.

"Erin, what are you doing?" Kent blocked the box with his arm. "If it's what I said—"

"It's exactly what you said." Erin firmed her chin. "But you're right and it's okay. Let's take the whole box over to Wanda's right now and let her decide if any of these are worth selling."

Grinning, Kent began handing her baskets to repack.

When they finished, she glanced up meekly. "If you'll carry this one out to your pickup, I have another box-ful in the closet."

His knowing look said he wasn't surprised, but he kindly said nothing. Erin retrieved the second box, then detoured to the kitchen to grab her purse and house keys. Catching up with Kent outside, she waited while he secured both boxes in the pickup bed. Shortly, they were on their way downtown.

"Didn't waste any time, did you?" Wanda bestowed a vibrant smile upon Erin. "Let's see what you brought. We can use the table behind the register."

Kent set down the box and peeled back the flaps. When he handed Wanda the top two baskets, Erin could hardly breathe as she watched the shop owner exam-ine each one.

"Fine craftsmanship, and the artistic touches are stunning." Wanda set those baskets aside and reached into the box for another, then cast Erin a disbelieving frown. "I could shake you silly for not telling me about these the day I hired you."

Erin was already shaking plenty on her own. "H-how much do you think they'd sell for?"

"I'd need to confirm with a shop owner in Austin who knows more about baskets than I do, but offhand I'd say this larger one with the lid might go for fifty dollars or more."

"People would actually pay that much?"

Laughter exploded from Wanda's throat. "Honey, did you just fall off a turnip truck? Of course they would!" She peered deeper into the box. "Why, I'd estimate you have at least five hundred dollars' worth of basketry right here."

Gripping a chair back to brace herself, Erin hoped she wouldn't hyperventilate.

"We've got another box in my truck," she heard Kent say over the ringing in her ears.

"Well, bring 'em on in." Wanda was already setting the baskets out on the table. "We need to make an inventory list and take some pictures I can send my Austin colleague. I'll draw up a consignment contract, and once she gets back to me with pricing suggestions, we'll be set to go."

"Erin?" Kent lightly touched her shoulder. "You look like you need to sit down."

"Maybe I'd better." A stunned laugh bubbled through her chest as Kent helped her into a chair.

While Kent went out to his truck, Wanda began snapping photos with her cell phone. Between shots, she made notes as Erin described the materials and techniques she'd used to make each basket. Erin barely heard the door chime signaling Kent's return.

"Excuse me, but you've got customers," Kent told Wanda as he plopped the second box on the floor beside the table.

Wanda laid aside her phone. Beaming a smile, she strode around the counter. "Help you, ladies?"

Glancing toward the door, Erin recognized Sue Ellen Jamison and Janice Mussell, two women Marie Peterson had introduced her to at Bible study last Sunday. She tuned out their conversation and welcomed a few minutes to wrap her head around this promising new development.

Kent pulled out another chair and sat facing her. "You okay?"

"That's debatable."

A crooked grin creased his face. "What did I tell you, Erin? You've got an amazing talent."

Before she could respond, Wanda bustled over. "Honey, I know we haven't settled on terms yet, but do you mind if I show these ladies a few of your baskets?"

"Erin, you made these yourself?" Sue Ellen admired a small twig basket similar to the one Erin had designed for Avery's birthday. "Why, I just have to have this one for my granddaughter. How much is it?"

"You can see it's one of a kind." Wanda offered a persuasive smile. "And just look at the intricate design. You'd pay $70 or more for something like this in the city. But our price today is just $49.95."

Sue Ellen insisted she had to have the basket and whipped out her charge card. Erin struggled to hide her shock while Wanda rang up the purchase and wrapped the little basket in glittery tissue paper. When the ladies left the shop twenty minutes later, three of Erin's baskets left with them, each one for an amount that left Erin speechless and Kent beaming like he'd pulled off the coup of the century—which, in Erin's opinion, he certainly had.

"Alrighty now." Notebook in hand, Wanda pushed baskets aside and plopped into a chair on the other side of the table. "Let's get down to business on that consignment agreement."

Driving Erin home following their meeting with Wanda, Kent marveled at the change in her confidence level. He could only laugh to himself as she bubbled over with ideas. "Maybe my one-of-a-kind baskets could become the cornerstone of my own interior design business. I could call it Weaving Hearts and Homes or The Designer's Basket or—"

When he parked in her driveway, she turned to him with a panicked stare. "Oh, Kent, how selfish of me. I promised to help you with your house, and now all I can talk about are my own plans."

He shifted to reach for her hand, but the soft pressure of her fingertips almost made him forget what he meant to say. "Doing what makes you happy and ensuring a secure future for you and Avery are the only things that matter."

Erin offered a shivery smile, her blue eyes filling before she surprised Kent with a spontaneous hug. "How will I ever thank you for believing in me?"

For a split second, he sat frozen, unsure what to do with his hands. Before he could figure it out, Erin shrank back, her stunned gasp mirroring Kent's confusion. Yeah, it was unbelievable, all right. Unbelievable how he suddenly wanted to kiss this woman.

"I should go," he mumbled with a nervous laugh. "Need to get back to scraping and prepping."

"Right." Erin reached for the door handle. Another of those endearing coral blushes rose from her collar to her cheeks. "I'll look again at those paint samples and start on some interior design ideas."

Driving away, he suspected she'd give his home renovation project way more time and attention than she could spare, and in a crazy way, it made him happy. His mom would be all over his case, though. How many times had she pleaded with him to let her spruce up his place a bit? And how many times had he refused, saying he liked things plain and simple?

Well, there was *nothing* plain about Erin Dearborn. And nothing simple about the effect she had on him.

And the fact that he was good with that? Staggering.

* * *

Once Kent got started on the exterior repairs and painting prep, it hadn't taken him long to decide he could use help. Elijah was all too glad for the extra work and even brought along a couple of buddies. At the rate they were going, Kent expected to start painting by the weekend.

On Saturday morning, as he hauled out paint, rollers and brushes to get set up for his crew, Erin's car turned into the driveway. He set a five-gallon paint bucket down with a thud and massaged his shoulder on his way to greet her.

"Wow." Her gaze swept the side of the house, which now showed more weathered gray siding than old flaking paint. "You've been working hard."

"Can't take all the credit. I've had good helpers." Feeling grubby next to Erin's lacy white cotton blouse and dark-wash jeans, he dusted his hands against his pant legs. He hadn't even bothered to shave this morning.

Erin opened the back door for Avery. As the little girl climbed out, Erin went around to the trunk. "I brought some ideas to show you. Can you spare a few minutes?"

"Sure." Kent's brows shot up at the sight of the large burlap-covered board Erin lifted out. She'd used ribbon to divide the board into six areas representing each room of his house, each one containing sketches, magazine clippings and color swatches. He breathed out an appreciative whistle. "Talk about working hard."

"I helped," Avery said. "Mommy let me cut out pictures."

"And you did a great job." The board dwarfed Erin, so Kent offered to carry it. "Let's take this inside and y'all can tell me all about it."

Showing them to the living room, Kent propped the board in front of the TV and stepped back, then had to nudge Skip out of the way. "No dog slobber allowed, fella."

Erin moved next to the board. "Keep in mind these are only suggestions." A hint of nervousness tinged her voice. "If there's anything you don't like, please tell me."

"Like I'd have a clue." Kent grinned and rolled his eyes.

Her shoulders heaved with a steadying breath. "Since Mrs. Thompson didn't provide photos of the inside, I did a little research into the era when your house was built and imagined how it might have looked with a woman's touch."

Something that was sadly lacking, Kent had to admit. Since Skip and Avery had already claimed the easy chair like best buds, he backed up to sit on the sofa while Erin described her selections for each room. She was using words like *chintz* and *finial* and other terms that sounded like a foreign language to him, so he mostly smiled and nodded. Little as he understood about interior decorating, he was happy just listening to Erin's sweet voice, while his mind drifted to scenarios he had no business imagining.

Like coming in from ranch work to find her in the kitchen making supper for him and Avery.

Like cuddling with her on the sofa in the evenings while they watched a romantic movie on TV.

Like wishing he could walk into one of those rooms she was describing and find her there every day making her baskets.

"Kent? Did you hear me?"

He mentally shook himself and tried to recall the last

thing Erin had said. "Uh, yeah. White trim all around would look real pretty."

Her smirk said she'd caught him woolgathering. Good thing she couldn't read his mind. "I think we should do the downstairs first, don't you?"

"Sounds good. Just give me a few days to get the outside painting done." Kent came closer to admire each of the room designs Erin had put together. It made him a little sad to think he'd be the only one living here to enjoy the finished product—and more than a little edgy to imagine half of Juniper Bluff trooping through these rooms during the sesquicentennial tour.

The rattle and groan of Elijah's ancient Honda hatchback returned him to the present. "There's my painting crew. Guess I'd better get to work."

"We'll get out of your way, then." Erin motioned for Avery, who grumbled about having to say goodbye to Skip.

Kent hefted the idea board and followed them out to Erin's car. She popped the trunk and he carefully laid the board inside. "Meant to ask," he said. "How are basket sales going?"

Erin beamed. "We sold six more since Tuesday. And Wanda's taken a couple of special orders on her website. I've already been working on those."

"That's great. Anytime you need materials…"

"Actually, would you mind if I snooped around your pastures again one day soon?"

Kent narrowed one eye and tried to look stern. "Only with an escort." Then he smiled. "I'm around all day tomorrow if you and Avery want to come out. We could take the horses on a trail ride."

Avery danced a jig. "Can we, Mom?"

"No, honey. Tomorrow's Easter, remember? Uncle Greg is coming tonight so he can go to church with us in the morning." Looking up at Kent, she pulled her lower lip between her teeth. "If you don't have other plans, we'd love for you to join us. Christina Austin says Easter worship at Shepherd of the Hills is a glorious service."

Watching Elijah and his pals reset the scaffolding, Kent scratched his neck and tried to recall the last time he'd been to church for Easter services. Must have been after his last Afghanistan deployment. Following his discharge from the service, he'd lived with his parents temporarily, and no way was he getting out of going to church on Easter Sunday if his mom had anything to say about it. But he'd left worship feeling angrier than ever at God. After all the flag-covered caskets Kent had paid his respects to in drafty echoing airplane hangars, the pastor's hope-filled sermon about Christ's resurrection didn't go over real well.

"I'm cooking ham and sweet potatoes for Easter dinner. I'll have blueberry pie, too," Erin said, interrupting his gloomy train of thought. She glanced away. "But if you have too much to do here, I understand."

"I, uh…"

"Hey, Kent," Elijah hollered, "we're ready to get painting."

"Be right there." Still debating with himself, he puffed out his cheeks. He sure didn't want to be a downer for Erin on a day that clearly meant a lot to her, much less impose on her family time. But the compulsion to say yes was eating him alive, and it had less to do with another delicious home-cooked meal at Erin's table than the chance to spend even one more hour with her.

"You have a big day ahead." Erin nodded toward his

painting crew as she opened the car door for Avery. "I'll talk to you next week—"

"Yes."

Erin swung her head around. "Yes?"

"Yes, I accept your invitation. If it's still okay."

Her brows drew together. "For dinner, you mean?"

He was sure to regret this, but then he didn't seem to have a whole lot of control over his decisions these days. He choked down the boulder blocking his vocal cords. "I'll try to make it to church, too. What time does it start?"

The spark in those gorgeous blue eyes kindled a blaze beneath Kent's heart. "Worship starts at ten thirty, but we'll already be there for Sunday school. I'll watch for you and save you a seat."

With a brisk nod, Kent got Erin's door for her. As she buckled her seat belt, she sent him a smile filled with hope and happiness, and the knowledge that he'd put it there made his chest swell with his own kind of joy.

Come tomorrow morning, he knew what he absolutely *could not do*—chicken out. Erin might understand and forgive him, but he'd never forgive himself.

As Erin drove away, he clenched his jaw and offered up the first prayer he'd prayed in too long to remember. *This one's on You, Lord. I may be doing the hard work of fixing up my house, but if You want me back, You're gonna have to do an even bigger renovation of my heart.*

Chapter Eight

After tucking Avery into bed Saturday night, Erin brought down the bag of goodies she'd hidden away in her closet for Avery's Easter basket.

As she spread everything out on the coffee table, her brother Greg muted the basketball game he was watching. "Went all out, didn't you? Sure Avery isn't going to OD on chocolate?"

Erin laughed, "Probably." She adjusted the big pink bow attached to the basket handle, then arranged green yarn to line the inside. Pondering a chocolate bunny, she pursed her lips. "Maybe I did go a little overboard. But with all Avery's been through this past year—"

"With all you've *both* been through," Greg interrupted. He looked away and murmured, "I only wish you pressed charges."

"All I wanted was to get away and put it all behind me." Erin arranged the chocolate bunny in Avery's basket. "Besides, I didn't want anyone to know what a huge mistake I'd made."

Greg offered an understanding smile as he handed her a bag of tiny candy eggs. "This actually makes me kind of sorry my daughter's all grown-up now and too big to make an Easter basket for."

"Taylor's driving over from College Station in time for church tomorrow, right? Make her a basket. I've certainly got chocolate to spare. Baskets, too," she added with a wink.

"You talked me into it. If nothing else, it'll give Taylor another reason to suspect her dad's gone bonkers."

"That hasn't been officially confirmed yet?" Erin elbowed her brother in the ribs before marching to her workroom.

After selecting a basket she thought Taylor would like, she grabbed another skein of green yarn. When she returned to the family room, Greg had filled several plastic eggs with loose change and little candies. He glanced up with a grin. "This is really bringing back memories."

Reclaiming her spot on the sofa, Erin set the basket and yarn in front of Greg. "I'm glad you and Taylor have such good memories of Vivienne. She was a wonderful woman."

"That she was." The faraway look in her brother's eyes spoke of how much he still missed his late wife.

Erin touched his knee. "You're not too old to marry again and have more kids."

"Ha. Not likely." Greg slanted a meaningful look in her direction. "But you, on the other hand…"

"I totally failed at one marriage. I'm nowhere near ready to try again."

"You aren't the one who failed."

Dropping her chin, Erin released a sigh. "My head gets it. My heart? Not so much." She picked up one of the plastic eggs Greg had filled. Coins and candy rattled inside, bringing a smile to her face. "This is kind of what my life feels like now. Every day, a new surprise inside, and I have to say, lately they've mostly been good surprises."

Greg unwrapped one of the chocolate eggs and popped it into his mouth. "Like a certain rancher handyman who'll be joining us tomorrow?"

Flames seared Erin's cheeks. "Kent doesn't have any family close by, and I hated the thought of him spending Easter all by himself."

"Mmm-hmm." Greg unmuted the TV. With one eye on the game, he arranged plastic eggs and candies in Taylor's basket.

Giving a huff, Erin returned her attention to Avery's basket. She finished it off with a miniature pink velvet bunny. Then, having enough of both a basketball game that she had no interest in and her brother's allusions to a nonexistent romance, she decided to get a head start on tomorrow's dinner preparations.

Problem was, thinking about the dinner menu only made her more aware of the guest she'd invited. Greg's teasing aside, Erin couldn't deny there was *something* going on between her and Kent. But how could she possibly risk opening her heart to a man on the run from God?

Except…he'd as much as promised to be at church in the morning, which had to mean there was hope. Whether anything more came of their friendship or not, she'd pray for the Lord to restore Kent's faith.

Kneeling backward on the pew, Avery peered toward the foyer. "I don't see him yet, Mom."

"I'm sure he's coming." Not the least bit sure at all,

Erin tried her best not to turn around and look for herself. The worship service would begin in less than five minutes, and the praise team already had everyone on their feet singing. The whole sanctuary reverberated with voices and instruments raising joyous Easter hallelujahs.

Erin's niece, Taylor, leaned past Avery and spoke over the music. "That lost-looking guy standing way over there against the wall—could he be your friend?"

Looking in the direction Taylor indicated, Erin spotted Kent near the sanctuary entrance. Lips mashed together, hat held at his waist like a shield, he looked as if he'd rather be anywhere else.

But he'd come!

Hoping to reach him before he decided to duck out, Erin edged from the pew. She approached shyly, fearful of startling him. "Hi. You made it."

He blinked several times, like a man coming out of a trance. "Didn't know it would be so crowded." An uneasy smile crept across his face. "Or so loud."

"You know what they say—it's one of those Sundays when all the CEOs show up."

"CEOs?"

"Christmas-and-Easter-only Christians. It's okay, though," Erin added quickly. "God's arms are always open in welcome. He's glad you're here. And so am I."

Kent's darting gaze settled fully on Erin, and a tiny bit of his tension seemed to lift. "Is there a term for somebody like me who hasn't darkened a church door in years?"

"Yes," Erin replied with a firm nod. "God's forgiven and dearly loved child." She boldly linked her arm through his. "Come sit with us. Avery's been watching for you ever since Sunday school let out."

Returning to her family, Erin made room for Kent, strategically placing him between herself and Avery in case he got any ideas about bolting. She needn't have worried, though. As Pastor Terry read the Easter gospel, she glanced over to see Kent's chin trembling. Acting as if his eye itched, he flicked away a drop of moisture. Knowing he'd be embarrassed to think she'd noticed, she resisted the compulsion to hand him a tissue from her purse.

Then she glimpsed Avery slide her tiny hand into Kent's and give it an encouraging squeeze. Now Erin was the one in need of a tissue. Keeping her gaze forward, she quietly blew her nose and pretended it was the Easter message that had moved her to tears—and truthfully, it was, because she certainly felt as if she'd witnessed the beginnings of a heart redeemed through Christ's love.

When worship ended, the Austins, Willoughbys and several other friends stopped to say hello but kindly didn't make a big deal about the fact that they hadn't seen Kent in church before. Both Christina and Diana sent meaningful looks in Erin's direction, though. They'd probably be peppering her with questions at the first chance they got.

Near the main doors, Pastor Terry greeted them. When Erin introduced Kent, Pastor Terry offered his hand in a hearty shake. "Yes, I've seen you around town, Kent. Welcome, and happy Resurrection Sunday."

"Thanks." Tensing again, Kent cleared his throat. His voice dropped to a murmur. "Would it be okay if I came by to talk one day this week?"

Pastor Terry's brows twitched upward in a gratified smile. "Give me a call anytime."

As they stepped outside, Erin motioned for Greg to

take Taylor and Avery on to the car. Walking a little farther with Kent, she shielded her eyes from the bright sun overhead. "See you at the house in a few minutes?"

With the straw Western hat shading his face, it was hard to make out his expression. "Yeah, I'll be along."

"If this morning has been too much for you, I'll understand."

"No, it's okay. I just need a couple minutes." He looked up toward the steeple.

As Erin followed his gaze, her heart threw in an extra beat at the sight of the shimmering metal cross against a crystal blue sky. "That's a view—and a reminder—I'll never get enough of." At Kent's nod and brief smile, she drew a quick breath. "Well, take your time. We'll see you when you get there."

She left Kent standing on the church's front walk and hurried over to Greg's SUV. She climbed into the back next to Avery and slumped into the seat cushion.

"Everything okay?" Greg asked as he started the engine.

"I think so." Erin glimpsed Kent slowly making his way toward his pickup at the far edge of the parking lot. He still looked lost in thought. "Maybe you could tell Kent's working through some stuff."

As traffic cleared, Greg headed toward the street. "Seth told me he served in Afghanistan. Had to be tough."

In the front passenger seat, Taylor tucked a short blond curl behind her ear before slipping on tortoiseshell sunglasses. "He sure is one cute cowboy." She grinned over her shoulder. "If I were you, Aunt Erin, I wouldn't let him get away."

Erin stiffened. "We're just friends."

"Mmm-hmm." Taylor glanced back at Avery. "What do *you* think of him, cuz?"

"He's nice." Avery stroked the ears of her new stuffed bunny. "He has horses and cows and a big dog that sleeps in his chair."

Taylor laughed, "Wow, that must be one huge chair!"

"No kidding," Greg chimed in. "With all the live-stock camped out in his living room, no wonder the guy's still single."

"Enough, you two." Erin punched the backs of Greg's and Taylor's seats, which only made them both laugh harder.

While Avery painstakingly explained that only Skip the dog lived in Kent's house, Erin tuned them out. Maybe if she concentrated on the dinner preparations she still needed to make, she could stop dwelling on Kent Ritter and the unnerving jumble of emotions his mere presence always seemed to evoke.

Kent sat in his pickup for several long minutes after the parking lot had cleared. He'd come to church this morning mainly to keep his word to Erin. Never in a million years had he expected the service to affect him so profoundly. *Called or not called, God is present*, Erin had quoted the first time she'd shared a meal with him. Now it felt like God was doing the calling, and it scared Kent silly. He'd certainly surprised himself when he'd asked about meeting with the pastor, but it seemed like the next logical step. All these years of pretending he *didn't* need to talk about Afghanistan—worse, pretending he didn't need God—and all it had taken to crack his armor was the faith of one caring and beautiful woman.

Careful, Ritter. You just might be falling for the girl.

That was a puzzle for another day. As his dad always said, best not to put the cart before the horse. Kent needed to get his own life in order before he brought anyone else into it—especially Erin and her sweet little daughter. When Avery had taken his hand this morning, he'd almost lost it for real. He could still feel the tender compassion in the touch of those tiny fingers.

With a loud sniff, he worked on pulling himself together. Not a good idea to keep his hostess waiting. Besides, several hours had passed since his 5:00 a.m. bowl of cereal before morning chores. He felt like he could almost smell Erin's ham and sweet potatoes from here.

When he parked in her driveway a few minutes later, Greg and the young woman Erin had introduced as her niece, Taylor, were sneaking around the front flower beds hiding eggs.

Greg ambled over, a basket handle draped over his arm. "Just in time. We could use some help."

"Sure." Whipping off his hat, Kent had Greg transfer as many colored eggs as the upturned crown would hold.

As he concealed his last egg at the base of the mailbox post, Erin stepped onto the porch. Her face lit up when she saw him. "Dinner's on the table, guys. Let's eat first, and Avery can have her egg hunt afterward."

"All this for one little girl?" Kent smirked as he followed Greg and Taylor up the porch steps. Meeting Erin's gaze, he added, "I have to admit, she's a pretty special kid."

"I think so, too." Erin's eyes said so much more than her words.

So she'd noticed his reaction in church. He checked

himself to see how he felt about it and realized he was amazingly okay.

"Hurry up, Aunt Erin," Taylor called from the dining room. "I'm starving!"

Erin showed Kent to the table. "Avery begged for you to sit next to her."

"It'd be my pleasure."

Nearly an hour later, with his stomach on the verge of exploding, Kent still couldn't bring himself to refuse a second slice of blueberry pie. As Erin refilled his coffee cup, he looked up with an appreciative smile. "If you ever tell my mother I said so, I'll deny it to my dying day, but your cooking beats hers by light years."

Erin's eyes sparkled. "I hope I get to meet her someday."

Avery tugged on her mother's sleeve. "Can I have my Easter egg hunt now?"

Perfect timing, before Kent let his guard down even further.

Avery dashed to the family room and returned with her Easter basket. "Let's go, Mom. Come on, Mr. Ritter. You can help me look."

Letting himself be dragged toward the front lawn, Kent glanced back at Erin with a helpless shrug. "Guess I've been drafted."

After all the eggs were found and Kent had helped with the kitchen cleanup, he decided he should leave the rest of the afternoon to Erin and her family. As she walked him to the door, he thanked her again for including him. "Best Easter I've had in a long, long time."

"You made the day special for us, too," she said. "In case you haven't noticed, Avery's really taken with you. She can be apprehensive around men outside the family."

"I'm honored to have passed the Avery test." He jingled his truck keys. "Better hit the road. Still got chores to do."

Erin looked at him askance. "Not planning on doing more painting on Easter Sunday, I hope."

"No way!" Not that he wouldn't have done just that if Erin hadn't invited him today, but this was better by a long shot. "The boys and I made good progress yesterday, but horses and cattle don't take holidays. Can't let 'em go hungry."

"No, I guess not." Concern narrowed Erin's smile as she studied him. "Will you be okay?"

Taking her meaning, Kent nodded. "Yeah. I'm pretty sure I will be."

"Good. I'll keep praying for you."

"Thanks." He shot her a wink. "And save me some egg salad in case a doorknob gets loose or another shelf collapses."

"I will." Her laughter rang out, and the sweet sound echoed through his thoughts all the way home.

Chapter Nine

"Thanks for stopping by, Mrs. Glazer," Erin said as she walked her customer to the door. The woman's purchases included one of Erin's decorative fruit baskets, plus she'd asked for Erin's advice about redoing her living room. "Call me later this week and I'll come over to take a look."

Wanda beamed as she strode around the front counter. "Girl, I'm telling you, with your eye for design and my business savvy, just imagine the possibilities. We could change the name of the shop to Interiors by Wanda and Erin."

"Or Erin and Wanda," she quipped over her pounding pulse. Her boss couldn't be serious… Could she? Erin might have dreams of launching her own interior design company, but the logistics intimidated her like crazy. Her talents lay in artistry and design, not business and marketing. Partnering with an established career woman like Wanda Flynn could make all the difference.

"Oh, and by the way, here's another special order for a basket." Wanda handed her the email she'd printed out.

"This lady has a knitting shop over in Fredericksburg and wants a specially designed basket for toting supplies."

Erin scanned the message. The buyer wanted a soft-sided, tightly woven basket with an interior pocket and handles, and she'd included a copy of the shop logo for Erin to work into the design. "Wow, I've never done anything quite this involved."

Wanda patted Erin's arm. "I have confidence in you, sweetheart. Let me give you an advance to buy supplies." She opened the cash drawer. "And why don't you take off a little early today so you can get started?"

"Maybe I should," Erin murmured as she mentally reviewed her schedule. She'd already made plans to shop with Christina this afternoon. Plus, she'd offered to go out to Kent's tomorrow after work to help him paint his kitchen. How did life get so busy all of a sudden?

Leaving the shop shortly before noon, she hoped Kent would still be at the hardware store. As she parked, he came out pushing a gas grill on wheels and lined it up with others already on display.

"Gearing up for barbecue season, I see." Erin ambled over and tried to ignore the flutter of anticipation, a sensation all too common around Kent these days.

His welcoming smile only intensified the feeling. "Don't you know it's *always* barbecue season in Texas? Anyway, these are last year's models. Need to make room for the new ones." He gestured toward the closest one, doing a convincing imitation of a used-car salesman. "This could be yours for the low, low price of only $89.95."

"Not in my budget, even on sale, I'm afraid—although, at the rate things are going, that could change." Erin described her eventful morning at the shop. "Wanda had to have been joking about the partnership."

"Wouldn't be so sure." Kent's encouraging smile warmed her. "You're without a doubt the best interior designer I've ever known."

Grinning, she narrowed one eye. "And how many would that be, exactly?"

His grimace told the tale.

"That's what I thought," Erin said with a snicker. Growing serious, she continued, "I'd really hoped to help paint your kitchen tomorrow, but with everything else that's come up—"

"Don't think twice about it. I'll manage just fine."

"Are you sure? Because I feel like I'm letting you down."

"You're not." Kent lightly touched her wrist, his voice softening. "You never could."

A tingle raced up Erin's arm as she smiled her thanks. "While I'm shopping with Christina this afternoon, I'll take your color samples and look at kitchen curtain fabric."

"You're planning to sew the curtains yourself?"

"I'm a woman of many talents," she said with a twitch of her brow, and realized it was true. Basket maker, seamstress, interior designer—it was only a matter of finding the confidence to make the best use of those talents.

Finding Kent gazing at her, a crooked grin skewing his lips, she tilted her head. "What?"

"You." His grin widened. "The first time I saw you in my pasture under the tree, you reminded me of a scared little rabbit trying hard to act brave. It's good to see it's not so much of an act anymore."

A sense of pride rippled through her. "It helps to have encouraging friends who believe in me."

Kent grew silent, his gaze shifting briefly toward the road. He glanced back at her, the corners of his eyes narrowing. "I think you've helped me more. If not for you, I doubt I'd have set foot in a church again, much less sat down for a one-on-one with the minister."

"Oh, Kent." Erin's eyes welled, and she instinctively reached for his hand. "Did you talk to Pastor Terry? How did it—" Shaking her head, she clamped her lips together. "I'm sorry. It's none of my business."

"Don't you dare apologize for caring." Tenderly, he cradled her hand with both of his. "It's one of the things I lo—" His throat worked. "What I mean is, you're a good friend and I'm grateful to have you in my life."

Nerves thrumming, she could barely breathe. "I feel the same way."

The door opened behind them. When Ben Zipp ambled out, Erin and Kent sprang apart, arms dropping to their sides.

"Great sale on grills, young lady." Offering a perceptive grin, Ben stroked a shiny black lid. "Hope my hotshot salesman here is answering questions to your satisfaction."

"Doin' my best." Kent ducked his head.

Erin edged toward her car. "Actually, I need to be going." So much for acting brave. "I'll get back to you about the…the curtains and such."

Driving away, she replayed their conversation, especially the moment when she felt sure Kent had almost used the word *love*. He'd probably only meant it as a figure of speech, but it said a lot about how much their friendship had grown.

She certainly couldn't deny the changes in herself in the short time she'd lived in Juniper Bluff. When Greg had first suggested the move, she'd been terrified of living on her own as a single mom. Even with Greg and his money as her safety net, she'd had doubts she could manage it. Yet, that was exactly what she was doing, and every day it got a little easier.

"I *am* a woman of many talents," she said aloud. Hearing the self-assurance in her voice, she sat up a little straighter behind the wheel. "And when God shows me the time is right—and the *man* is right—I'll be ready to open my heart again."

Kent Ritter's face instantly popped into her thoughts. This…whatever it was between them…was both wonderful and terrifying. *One step at a time*, she reminded herself. For now, she'd simply enjoy their friendship while praying for Kent to find his way back to the Lord.

Kent glared at his boss—a friendly glare but not altogether forgiving. "Thanks for nothing, Ben."

"Gotta keep my employees honest." Ben adjusted the big red-and-white sale tag on one of the grills.

"I *was* being honest, in case you didn't notice." At least, he'd been about to be. Kent had suffered the strongest urge to confide in Erin, and not only about his visit with Pastor Terry.

Ben clapped him on the back, fatherly affection in the older man's eyes. "Told you the other day there's a right time for everything, didn't I?"

"Yeah. So?"

"So be sure you're at peace with yourself before you pass the point of no return with that sweet little gal." With a jerk of his chin, Ben marched inside.

Point of no return? Kent pinched the back of his neck. Was he closer to that moment than he realized? He'd met Erin barely three weeks ago, and considering they were both wounded souls, it would be foolish and dangerous to rush into anything resembling romance. Erin's confidence might be blooming with each new opportunity, and Kent was definitely seeing his life in a new light after his conversation with Pastor Terry, but he still had a lot of healing to do.

Problem was, the deeper his feelings grew for Erin, the more impatient with himself he became. He whipped out his cell phone and tapped Pastor Terry's number. When the pastor picked up, Kent identified himself and said, "I know we talked about meeting again next week, but could we maybe do it sooner? Like…today?"

"How about lunch? Want to meet at Casa Luis?"

"That'd be great. I'm about to finish up at the hardware store."

There was a pause. "You okay, Kent? Did something happen?"

"Not really. But I could use some help putting a few things into perspective."

"I'll say an extra prayer for the Holy Spirit to enter into our discussion."

Kent spent the drive to the restaurant framing the thoughts and questions he wanted to share with Pastor Terry. Mainly, he needed to believe he wasn't too damaged to become the kind of man deserving of a woman like Erin.

Over their combo plates of tamales, enchiladas, rice and beans, Pastor Terry assured him of just that. "Yes, your time in Afghanistan and everything you experienced there left scars. But you were a good man before your military service, and you are a good man now. Above all else, you are still a beloved child of God."

"That's one thing I'm struggling with." Kent stabbed a bite of enchilada. "I've been angry with God for so long, blaming Him for this messed-up world where human beings maim and kill each other in senseless power struggles. Makes it hard to believe His love makes a difference."

"It does, though. God's love, working through people like you, makes a difference because you care enough to strive for—even *fight* for—a better world."

Letting the pastor's words sink in, Kent scooped guacamole onto a tortilla chip and studied it. "Think we'll ever be able to look back and see the difference we made?"

"That's where faith comes into play, because while our human vision is limited, our eternal God knows how the story ends, and He has already declared it good." Pastor Terry cast a regretful glance at his watch. "Unfortunately, I need to get to my next appointment. But let's talk again soon, okay?" Sliding from the booth, he snatched up both their checks and offered a warm smile. "See you in church next Sunday."

Not a question, not an invitation. Kent nodded, figuring he owed the pastor another Sunday since he'd just treated Kent to lunch.

More than that, he owed it to himself. If Ben Zipp was right about there being a time for everything, then this must be Kent's time for getting right with God. So he'd come down to two choices: continue wandering in his spiritual desert, or go all in with this faith thing and watch what the Lord could do with a committed life.

Pulling up next to his house later, he was struck

again by what a difference a fresh coat of white paint had made. He also knew from the work he and the boys had put in that it wasn't merely superficial. They'd filled in cracks, nailed down loose siding, replaced broken shutters—whatever repairs were needed to create a clean and intact surface for painting. Seemed like the ideal metaphor for the work Kent faced in shoring up his spiritual life.

When he rode out to check on his cattle, he found one of the cows with her new calf already on its feet and nursing—a good sign. Typically, it was the bred heifers he had to worry about, since this would be their first experience calving. It might be a blessing in disguise that only a few were pregnant this year, because this hurry-up renovation project was keeping him busy enough, and he didn't need any other problems.

Returning to the house, he got busy on the kitchen. He patched a few holes in the plaster and taped off the woodwork, then spread a tarp across the floor before pouring paint into a roller pan. The creamy yellow Erin had selected made him smile as the dreary room brightened with every stroke of the paint roller.

Skip was smart enough—or lazy enough—to stay in the living room and out of Kent's way. Until supper time anyway, when the dog plopped his rear down on the tarp and gave Kent "the look."

"Leave it to a hungry dog to let a guy know when it's quitting time." Kent chuckled as he covered the paint and wrapped the roller in a plastic bag.

While Skip crunched his kibble, Kent grilled a pork chop for himself and heated a can of mixed veggies. He ate his meal in front of the TV and had just set the plate aside when his cell phone rang. When he read Erin's name on the display, his pulse ramped up a notch.

"Hope I'm not interrupting anything," she said.

"Just kicking back with Skip. We were painting most of the afternoon."

"We?"

"Skip's my CEO—canine executive officer." With her gentle laughter wrapping around him like a cozy blanket, Kent settled back against the sofa cushions. "How was your trip to Fredericksburg?"

"Quite successful. Which is why I'm calling. I found the perfect curtain fabric for your kitchen and I can't wait to show you. Can I bring it out tomorrow after work?"

"I thought you needed to start on the special-order basket."

"I'll go blind if I spend the whole afternoon on it. What if I drop by before I pick up Avery from school? I'll bring the fabric swatch and also measure the windows."

"Sounds good." Inhaling deeply, Kent sat forward, forehead braced in his hand. "Erin, about this morning at the store, I know things were starting to get awkward, and I just wanted to say…" Actually, he had no idea where he was going with this.

A muffled sigh. "It's okay, Kent. You don't have to explain."

But he did. Scrambling for words, he rushed on, "The thing is, you've been on my mind all day. Practically since we first met, to tell the truth. And it's making me wonder—"

"Kent. Stop." Her tone was gently insistent. "There are things I'd like to say to you, too, but not over the phone. How about we table this discussion until I see you tomorrow?"

He didn't know if he could wait that long, but he recognized the wisdom of her suggestion. "Sounds good."

They said goodbye, and he tossed the phone onto the end table. As he massaged his eye sockets, Skip crawled off the easy chair and poked his nose under Kent's arm.

"Yeah, boy, I've got it bad." A strangled laugh burst from his throat. Scratching the old dog behind the ears, he shook his head at the crazy new direction his life had taken and prayed for the faith to believe God wouldn't let him go astray.

Seeing Kent's house for the first time with its new coat of paint made Erin's heart lift. She stood with her mouth agape and a hand to her throat.

Kent emerged from the back door, Skip trotting alongside. He came up next to Erin and looked toward the house. "What do you think?"

"I think it's amazing." She slanted him a reproving smirk. "Tell me it doesn't make you wish you'd started this project a long time ago."

"Guess I just needed the right incentives. With my place soon to be an official historical site, I scraped up enough to put a down payment on that bull I've had my eye on. This time next year, I'm hoping for some top-dollar calves."

Erin shrugged. "Getting a tax break is nice, but it should be incentive enough that this is your home." She instantly regretted her judgmental tone. "That's just me, though. I've always needed my home to be a pleasant, inviting place. It makes everything else more bearable."

A guilty look crinkled the corners of his eyes. "I'm beginning to think you might be right about that."

She looked up at him. "Really?"

"Yeah, really." A lazy smile warmed his features. "Want to see how the inside's coming along?"

"Yes!"

After grabbing her purse from the car, Erin walked with Kent to the house. As he held open the door to the screen porch, Skip darted in ahead of them.

Pausing at the threshold to the kitchen, Kent suggested, "Maybe you should close your eyes first."

Excitement coursed through her veins. She squeezed her eyes shut. "Okay, but don't let me trip on anything."

Kent's hand surrounded hers in a gentle but protective hold as he tugged her forward. "Little step up here. Now straight ahead." After a few more steps, he told her to open her eyes. "Ta-da!"

Erin gasped. The pastel yellow she'd selected from a tiny color sample card now bathed Kent's kitchen in the happy glow of a sunny day. "I love it!"

"It'll look even better once I get the trim painted." Kent took her hand again. "Already started on the living room. Come tell me what you think."

With the furniture moved to the center of the room and covered with old sheets, it didn't look much like a living room at the moment, but the two walls Kent had painted a light cocoa brown added charm and character.

"I can't believe how much you've done already. It looks great!" Erin eyed the scruffy dog curled up on the sheet covering an equally scruffy chair. "Have you thought about investing in some new furnishings to enhance the look?"

"Thought I'd leave that to my interior designer." Kent

winked. "So long as she remembers I'm a poor, hard-working cowboy."

"A cowboy who'd rather spend his hard-earned money on a prize bull," she said with a snort. "And before I forget what I came for…" She reached into her purse for the swatch of yellow calico she'd picked up at the fabric store. "Here's what I'd like to use for the kitchen curtains."

"Pretty." Kent fingered the cloth, but he was looking straight at Erin. "Real pretty."

Her pulse thrummed along either side of her throat. "Kent… I need to say something."

His mouth tightened into a strained smile. "Why don't I like the sound of that?"

Erin motioned toward the sheet-covered sofa. "Suppose we could sit down and talk for a minute?"

After Kent tossed aside the sheet, they each claimed an end of the sofa. Erin tucked one leg under her, hands clutched in her lap. "After what I went through with my ex-husband, I promised myself I'd never risk going through that again—for my own sake, but especially for Avery's."

"Nobody can blame you for that."

"There's more, though." Her voice dropped to barely above a whisper. "Kent, I like you a lot, and you're a wonderful friend. But the next time I give my heart to someone, he'll have to be a man I can trust completely. A man of faith. A man who's right with God."

Silence cloaked the room, the only sound Skip's rumbling snores as he dozed on the easy chair.

"I get it," Kent said with a shaky laugh. "I'm still finding my way through some stuff, and the last thing I want is to complicate your life with my baggage."

Erin scoffed. "Baggage? I've got truckloads." She tilted her head to meet his gaze with a reassuring smile. "But God is big enough and strong enough to bear it all. You just have to trust Him."

He reached for her hand. "Maybe you could pray for a little more of your faith to rub off on me."

"Already have been." She brushed at a streak of wetness on her cheek. "Now, why don't we take those curtain measurements before I have to pick up Avery from school?"

Chapter Ten

Kent really should have thought harder about under-
taking a major home-improvement project during spring
calving season. Three of his cows had delivered over
the weekend, and while the mamas and calves were
thriving, he'd grown concerned about a feisty little
heifer due any day now. Late Friday, he'd moved her
to a holding pen close to the barn so he could keep a
sharp eye on her.

His concerns proved justified when he found her
in labor early Sunday morning. He placed a quick call
to Doc Ingram, and within twenty minutes, the vet's
pickup nosed up to the pasture gate.

"Yep, she's struggling," Doc Ingram said as he joined
Kent inside the enclosure. "Let's move her into the barn
to a calving stall."

Once they were able to calm the heifer, the delivery
proceeded without complications, but the animal didn't
have a clue what to do with her newborn.

Kent peered into the stall where they'd moved the
scrawny black calf. "Looks like I'm gonna be bottle-
feeding."

Doc Ingram finished washing up at the barn sink. "Got some formula on hand?"

"Enough to get through the next couple of days. I'll pick up more while I'm in town tomorrow." Kent followed the vet out to his pickup. "Thanks, Doc. Sorry I had to get you up at the crack of dawn on a Sunday."

"All part of the job." With a quick glance at his watch, Doc Ingram grinned. "Still time to make it home for a shower and shave before church."

Church—Kent had nearly forgotten. Except now he had an abandoned calf to feed. So much for his promise to Pastor Terry, and to himself. Watching the vet drive away, Kent wondered if God gave credit for good intentions. On the other hand, he remembered enough about his Bible to know God didn't operate on the credit system. In fact, God's bookkeeping didn't make any kind of human sense at all, a good thing since Kent couldn't repay in a hundred lifetimes everything God had done for him in this one.

He'd sure counted on seeing Erin again today, though. As he mixed a batch of formula, he wondered if Erin would be watching for him to walk through the church doors. Avery, too, the cutie. Remembering how protective Erin's daughter had acted at first, Kent could hardly believe how she'd warmed up to him. He'd make sure Erin brought her out soon to see the calf.

An hour later, with the fuzzy little guy fed and nestled in a mound of clean straw, Kent went to the house to clean up and fill his own grumbling belly with the bowl of cereal he hadn't had time for until now. He'd just started out to the barn for another check on the cow and calf when Erin's dark blue sedan sped up the driveway.

She tumbled from the car, nearly tripping in her long

paisley skirt and dressy white sandals. "Kent, I was so worried! Are you okay?"

"I'm fine." Confused by her panic, he hurried over. "Would have called, but things got busy quick this morning."

Erin's gaze traveled from his face to his boot toes and back again. Her chest rose and fell in noisy gasps. "Then—then you're not hurt?"

"No," he assured her with a puzzled laugh. "What ever gave you that idea?"

By now, Avery had clambered from the back seat. She slid her hand into her mother's. "Mommy heard people talking about you at church."

"Diana Willoughby's husband," Erin supplied, still catching her breath. "And another man I thought was a doctor. It sounded like you'd been trampled by a cow and had to call for help."

"Uh, not exactly." Kent could no longer keep his laughter in check. "You do know Tripp Willoughby is a veterinarian, right? The other guy must have been Robert Ingram, Tripp's partner. I called Doc Ingram out early this morning for a high-strung heifer about to give birth."

Groaning, Erin covered her face. "A veterinarian. Now I feel like an absolute idiot."

Avery stepped closer and tugged on Kent's sleeve. "Is there a baby cow?"

"Sure is." Ignoring the whole "cows are girls and bulls are boys" explanation, he tweaked her earlobe. "Wanna see?"

"Oh, yes! Mommy, can I?"

Taking another gulp of air, Erin gave a weak nod.

"He's in the barn," Kent said, "around the corner to

the left. Be real quiet, okay? And stay outside the stall. Your mom and I will be along in a minute."

While Avery skipped toward the barn, Kent stooped for a closer look at Erin, relieved to see some of her color returning. An auburn curl had fallen across her cheek, and he tucked it tenderly behind her ear. "You were really that worried about me?"

"If I weren't such a dunce, I'd have asked for more details before rushing out." She swiveled just out of reach. "Besides, if you really had been in an accident, they might have taken you to the hospital and you wouldn't even have been here and—" Her voice broke.

"Erin, it's okay. *I'm* okay." Kent tucked her beneath his arm, pulling her close. She fitted so perfectly against his side—*too* perfectly. Her hair smelled of flowers and coconut, and he couldn't resist dropping a feathery kiss atop her head.

She relaxed slightly and pivoted to face him, her slim, delicate fingers resting on his chest. When she smiled up at him, it felt like a thousand arrows twanging through his heart. He was milliseconds away from kissing her, so close it would take wild horses and a herd of stampeding cattle to keep this from happening—

"Mom, you gotta come see!"

Or a precocious seven-year-old with the worst timing ever.

"Coming, honey." Erin's voice sounded an octave higher than normal. Shrugging out of Kent's embrace, she gave him a "this can't happen" look and strode purposefully toward her daughter.

Kent took a couple of jerky breaths while he brought his runaway emotions under control. Maybe the kid's timing wasn't so lousy after all. Hadn't Erin reminded him only days ago she couldn't let herself get involved with a man who didn't have his act together with the Lord? Kent might be making progress in that direction, but doubts and questions still ran rampant.

In the meantime, he had a bottle-fed calf and a half-finished house-painting job to worry about. Mashing his Resistol firmly on his head, he marched into the barn.

Around the corner, he came upon Erin and Avery gazing in wonder at the critter on the other side of the stall gate. Erin glanced his way, her gaze rapturous. "He's adorable. But shouldn't he be with his mother?"

"It'd be too dangerous." Kent explained how sometimes a cow just didn't take to her newborn and they had to be separated.

Chin resting on her folded arms, Avery nodded solemnly. "That's why my mom and I don't live with my dad anymore."

Kent's gut tightened. He cast Erin a searching look. "Did he ever—"

"No," she stated firmly. Sidling over to Kent, she kept her voice low. "Payne's abuse was always directed at me. I thank God every day for protecting Avery—and for getting us out of there before things got any worse."

When Erin turned away for another look at the calf, Kent let his imagination run wild with everything he'd like to do to Erin's ex. Men like Payne Dearborn ought to be locked up for life. But there'd never been any mention about pressing charges. Erin had only said she'd left him and filed for divorce. Maybe one day, when the time felt right and little ears weren't close by, he'd ask her more about it.

* * *

There were times, like just now, when Erin marveled at her young daughter's insight. She'd diligently tried to prevent Avery from witnessing Payne's abuse, but the aftereffects weren't so easily disguised. When Erin was so bruised and sore that she could barely endure holding her little girl in her lap, Avery always wanted to kiss away Mommy's "boo-boos." Even as a toddler, she'd snuggle in close with Erin and pat her back while she cried silent tears of pain and self-recrimination into her pillow. What a fool Erin had been to hope Payne would ever change.

Shaking off the memories, she called to Avery, "We should let the little guy rest, honey."

"But he's so cute, Mom." Avery cast Kent a hopeful smile. "Do you think I could help you feed him sometime?"

"If it's okay with your mom. But I don't think you want to be wearing your Sunday best."

Anticipation lit Avery's eyes. "We could go home and change clothes and then come back. When will he be hungry again?"

"Avery…" Erin shook her head.

"He'll need to eat every few hours for the first couple of days," Kent said, "and then twice a day after that until he's big enough to be weaned. So there'll be plenty of chances for you to give him a bottle."

"But when *today*?" Avery pressed.

Laughing, he winked at Erin, then glanced at his watch. "He should be ready for another bottle in an hour or two."

"See, honey," Erin said. "We have plenty of time to go home for lunch and change clothes."

Brows wiggling meaningfully, Avery grabbed Erin's wrist. "Or we could stay here and eat lunch with Mr. Ritter."

"Avery Dearborn." Erin gave an embarrassed huff. "You know it isn't polite to invite yourself to someone else's home for a meal."

"I don't mind," Kent murmured near Erin's ear, making her shiver. "But I have to warn you, it's pretty slim pickin's."

Trying hard to ignore her daughter's puppy-dog stare, Erin turned to Kent. "Are you sure?"

His gaze warmed. "If you're okay with BLTs and corn chips, I don't rightly see how I can say no to this pretty little lady."

"Yay!" Avery whisper-screamed the word while jumping up and down and silently clapping her hands.

"Good girl," Kent said. "Thanks for not waking our baby. Now, who's hungry?"

When Kent took Avery's hand and started out of the barn, Erin's eyes welled. *This*, she thought, following behind them, *is how a dad should treat his little girl.* Then Kent reached back for Erin's hand, his smile so tenderly reassuring, and her heart climbed into her throat. *This is how a good man treats the woman he cares for.*

Her thoughts returned to those moments before Avery had called to her from the barn. Kent had been about to kiss her, she was certain, and she would have let him. But once they crossed that bridge, it would be next to impossible to keep the promise she'd made to herself about staying uninvolved.

Her heart was telling her a different story, though, one with the happy ending she'd always dreamed of, even after Payne Dearborn had crushed her fantasies of a happily-ever-after with him. All she wanted now was to forget her first marriage had ever happened—except for the blessing of Avery that had come from it—and find out what God had in store in this new life He'd prepared for her.

Kent's big yellow dog bounding out the back door returned Erin's thoughts to the present. Skip headed straight for Avery and showered the girl with wet doggy kisses.

"Hey, boy! Are you so glad to see me? I missed you, too." Avery giggled and sank her fingers deep into the dog's ruff.

"Looks like y'all are gonna need a puppy soon," Kent teased as he motioned Erin into the kitchen.

Erin scoffed. "A puppy is way down my list of priorities at the moment." She paused to look around and saw that Kent had started painting the baseboards and window frames. The fresh coat of white made a perfect complement to the yellow walls. "You're nearly finished in here. Now I'm even more anxious to get the curtains done."

"Looks almost like a brand-new kitchen, doesn't it?" Kent patted the countertop. "At least the tiles are in pretty good shape. Replacing counters would be a bigger job than I have the time or the money for."

"These are fine. They may not be original to the house, but they're retro enough to lend some character."

Kent nodded and opened the fridge. "Guess we should get going with those BLTs."

While he fried the bacon, Erin sliced tomatoes and

separated lettuce leaves. Kent put Avery in charge of making toast. Soon, they sat down to lunch, and the moment they finished, Avery started asking when it would be time to feed the calf again.

"And you have to name him, too," she insisted.

Kent didn't do a very good job of hiding his grimace, and Erin could guess why. She touched Avery's shoulder. "Honey, ranchers tend not to name the cows they're going to sell."

Avery's pale brows drew together. "You mean you aren't going to keep him?"

"For a while, yes," Kent began. "But when he grows up—I mean, the time will come when—" He cast Erin a look of desperation.

She smiled her understanding and told her daughter they'd talk more about it later. After the dishes were washed and put away, Kent said he should probably check on the calf again and prepare another bottle.

"Can I help this time?" Avery pleaded.

Erin bit her lip. "We're still in our church clothes, honey."

"I have an idea," Kent volunteered. "You could wear one of my old T-shirts over your Sunday dress to keep it clean."

When Erin agreed, Kent went to his room and brought back a faded orange shirt with the local feed store logo on the back. Avery pulled it on over her head, and it easily covered her down to her knees.

"But what about my Sunday shoes?" Avery pointed to her white patent leather sandals.

"Thought of that, too." Kent produced a pair of dingy tube socks with holes in the toes. "These were going in the trash anyway, so you can slip 'em on over your shoes."

Avery plopped down on the floor to pull on the socks. She looked up at Erin. "Mommy, what about you?"

"I'll just watch this time." Which was perfectly fine with her.

Not that she wouldn't have enjoyed helping, but for the present, she took great joy in watching the interaction between her daughter and Kent—his patience as he explained to Avery how he mixed the formula, his gentle guidance as he showed her how to hold the bottle at just the right angle while he steadied the calf.

"Mom," Avery cheered as she fed the calf. "I'm doing it!"

Peering over the stall gate, Erin beamed. "Yes, you are, honey. Good job."

"I wish we lived on a ranch. It would be so fun to pet the animals every day."

Kent grunted as the calf squirmed in his arms. "Ranching's hard work, Avery. Animals need tending day in and day out, even when you're tired or sick."

Avery grew quiet for a moment while the calf nursed, but the wheels were obviously turning in her seven-year-old brain. Lips puckering, she studied Kent. "But you live all alone. Who takes care of Skip and the horses and cows if you get sick?"

"Well, the good news is I don't get sick very often. But when I do, or if I need to be out of town for a couple of days, I have some real nice neighbors who don't mind pitching in."

The calf finished the bottle, and Kent led Avery out of the stall and latched the gate. Turning back for another peek, Avery said, "I still think he needs a name."

Kent shared a what-can-you-do look with Erin. "Then I think you should give him one."

"Let's see…" Avery placed a finger to her lips. "I think his name should be…Prince."

Erin laughed, "Prince? Why did you pick that name, honey?"

"Because he's a boy and because princes have servants and always get treated really special."

"Sounds like the perfect name to me." Kent bowed toward Avery. "Guess that means I should start calling you Princess."

"She certainly is that," Erin agreed. "Waited on hand and foot by her adoring mother, treated with extra special attention every day of her life."

Avery looked up with a winsome, wide-eyed gaze to rival the little calf's. "I wish you had someone to treat you special like a princess," she murmured, then added in a whisper, "like Mr. Ritter."

Erin's heart thudded. If Kent had overheard, he didn't acknowledge it, but headed to the workstation with the empty formula bottle.

"Honey," Erin said, dropping to one knee to better address her daughter, "you mustn't say things like that, especially around Mr. Ritter."

"Why not? He's nice to us, and I like him."

"I like him, too, but—" Erin made sure Kent was still busy with cleanup. "Such talk is very embarrassing to grown-ups, that's all. Now, I think it's time we say our goodbyes."

"Leaving already?" Kent stood a few steps away, his shirt and jeans spattered with soapy water.

Pushing to her feet, Erin dusted off her knee. She

forced a casual smile. "I still have more work to do on the knitting lady's basket, plus those curtains to sew."

"You're not taking on too much, are you?" Kent frowned with concern.

"I like keeping busy, especially with things I enjoy." Erin had Avery raise her arms so she could tug off Kent's T-shirt. "This afternoon was fun, though, and I'm glad we got to see the calf."

"Prince," Avery corrected. She handed Kent the grimy tube socks. "I hope we can visit him again soon."

"I hope so, too." Kent's gaze locked with Erin's, and he winked. "I think that would be very *special*."

Certain her face must be turning a million shades of red, Erin sent Avery to the house for her purse. Waiting at the car, she tried to look anywhere but at Kent—until he reached for her hand, and then she forgot how to breathe.

"You deserve to be treated like a princess," he said. "Always."

Avery's return rescued Erin from having to come up with anything more than a grateful nod in reply, since her brain seemed to have completely disconnected from her lips. "Well, bye," she managed, digging through her purse for her keys. "Thanks again for lunch. I—I'll call you when the curtains are ready."

Kent couldn't decide whether he wanted Erin to hurry up with the curtains or take her time. She'd no sooner driven away than he ached to see her again. On the other hand, he didn't exactly have his head on straight anytime they were together, and the last thing he wanted was to make a mistake. He'd meant every word when he told Erin she deserved to be treated like a princess.

He was no prince, but if he could ride in on his white steed—or black, actually, in Jasmine's case—and bring Erin a little happiness, he'd do it in a heartbeat.

In the meantime, he had plenty to distract him from such fanciful thoughts. Over the rest of Sunday afternoon and into the first part of the week, he finished painting the kitchen and living room, kept the calf fed, tended his horses and cattle, and put in his hours at the hardware store.

Passing Wanda's Wonders on his way home after his Wednesday morning shift, he couldn't resist stopping. He and Erin had spoken on the phone a couple of times since Sunday, but he'd been missing those sparkling blue eyes. Besides, he wanted to tell her he'd finished painting the downstairs woodwork last night and was ready to get started on the bedrooms.

As he ambled into the shop, he spotted Erin and a woman he didn't recognize deep in conversation near the counter, and neither of them looked happy. Protective instincts kicking in, he fought the urge to march to Erin's defense against what appeared to be a dissatisfied customer.

Feather duster in hand, Wanda emerged from the other side of a display case. "Wouldn't interrupt if I were you."

Kent pointed with his thumb toward the well-dressed Jennifer Lawrence look-alike. "Who is that?"

"Her name's Lauren Hall. She came in looking for Erin after seeing her baskets on the website."

"Then why does she look so upset?"

"Because," Wanda replied, mouth in a pucker, "she didn't drive all the way over from Dallas to buy a basket."

Kent pivoted to face the shop owner. "You obviously know what's going on here. So explain."

Before Wanda could respond, Erin's tearful voice carried through the shop. "No! No, I can't do it. I'm sorry, but I can't."

She charged for the door, only to draw up short when she saw Kent. Pausing only long enough to snatch a startled breath, she shook her head and ducked past him.

"Erin, wait." He grabbed for her arm but missed. The door banged shut behind her.

As Kent started after her, Wanda set her hand firmly against the door. "Give her some space. She's had a shock."

Kent tore his gaze from the door to stare first at Wanda, then at the stranger, who apparently was the cause of all this. She now stood a few feet away, her expression as distraught as Erin's had been.

Hands balled, Kent took a threatening step toward her. "Who exactly are you, and what did you say to Erin?"

The woman's chin shot up. "I don't think that's any of your business." Distractedly, she dug through her purse until she found a packet of tissues, then edged toward the door.

Kent blocked her path. "Erin's a friend of mine, so I'm making it my business. I'm asking again. What's this all about?"

A look came over her face that rocketed Kent back to the first time he saw Erin—the undercurrent of panic lurking beneath a mask of bravado.

He inhaled a calming breath and took a half step

back, palms raised. "I mean you no harm, ma'am. I'm just trying to understand what upset Erin so badly."

"It's all right, Lauren," Wanda said. "Kent here's real close with Erin. He may be able to help."

"Help with what?" What little patience Kent had mustered wouldn't last long. "One of you, please tell me what's going on."

The blonde dabbed a streak of mascara from beneath her eye. "Maybe you should ask Erin, since this is about her ex-husband."

The mention of Erin's abusive ex shot napalm through Kent's veins. "What about him? Has he done something?"

Silently, the woman reached one hand toward the filmy print scarf encircling her neck. Her eyes hardened, and with her gaze firmly fixed on Kent, she loosened the scarf. It fell away from her throat, exposing the greenish-yellow remnants of an ugly bruise.

Kent's stomach lurched. He felt like he might throw up. "Dearborn did this to you?"

"It happened two weeks ago after our engagement party. Because—silly me—I forgot to tell the caterers he despises crab cakes." She uttered a harsh laugh and held up her ringless left hand. "Needless to say, the engagement is off."

Turning away, Kent tried to get his breathing under control. When he faced Lauren Hall again, she'd retied the scarf. "I hate that he's done this to you," he said, "but I still don't get why you're here. Why would you want to put Erin through this again?"

"Because I need her help. Her testimony." Eyes flinty with determination, she stood straighter. "I'm pressing charges, but Payne's high-priced lawyers will use every trick in the book to get him off. If I can convince Erin to testify, it could keep the trial from devolving into a he said, she said farce—which I guarantee would give Payne the win."

While Kent digested this information, Wanda slid a comforting arm around Lauren. "You're doing the right thing, hon. And I'm sure Erin will come around, once she's had time to think things through."

Kent could only imagine the trauma Lauren Hall's request had dredged up for Erin. He needed to get to her. He needed to hold and comfort her. He needed her to know he'd do everything humanly possible to protect her from ever being hurt again.

Chapter Eleven

Why, God? Why now? Erin could barely see the road through her tears. She'd intended to go straight home, but then drove right past her turnoff. Unfamiliar scenery swept by in a blur, until she made herself pull over long enough to get her bearings and regain a semblance of control. With Avery getting out of school in a couple of hours, Erin didn't dare risk getting lost on country roads—or worse, spinning out and flipping the car into a ditch.

Spinning out of control pretty much described her feelings right now. Less than an hour ago, Mrs. Glazer had stopped in to ask if Erin would consult on redecorating her husband's insurance office—and offered a healthy fee. Afterward, Wanda had once again brought up the subject of a partnership, this time urging Erin to seriously consider the possibility. With her confidence soaring and the future looking brighter every day, the last thing she'd been prepared for was coming face-to-face with the new woman in Payne's life.

The initial twinge of jealousy had stunned her, then sickened her, before the feelings instantly evaporated.

She was done with Payne Dearborn. If anything, she felt sorry for Lauren Hall.

But not sorry enough to appear in court to relive ten years of Payne's increasingly cruel abuse.

She dropped her forehead against the steering wheel. "Forgive me, Lord. I just can't do it."

From deep inside her purse came the muffled ring of her cell phone. Much as she didn't feel like talking to anyone, she had to check in case it might be the school calling about Avery.

Kent's name flashed across the display, filling her mind with an image of his stricken face as she'd rushed out of Wanda's. Her voice shook as she answered. "Hi, Kent."

"Erin, are you okay?"

"I've just been driving. I had to get away."

"Where are you?" Urgency filled Kent's tone. "Please, you shouldn't be alone right now."

"I don't know, exactly. A few miles south of town." She glanced around. "There's a big iron gate with white stone pillars. I think it's someone's ranch."

A relieved sigh. "I know the place. Stay put. I'll be there in five minutes."

"But—"

"I mean it, Erin. You're in no shape to be driving. I'm coming for you." The line went dead.

She knew Kent was right. As proud as she'd been about growing more self-reliant, right now it would be welcome reassurance to have his strong shoulders to lean on. Making sure she was well to the side of the road, she shut off the engine and closed her eyes. She didn't even have the strength to pray.

Soon the rumble of tires on gravel sounded behind

her, and the grill of Kent's tan pickup filled her rearview mirror. Sitting up straighter, she blotted her cheeks with the damp tissue clutched in her fist.

Kent appeared at the passenger-side window. She hit the unlock button, and he slid into the seat. "Hey," he said with a concerned smile.

"Hey." She tried to smile back but couldn't keep her lower lip from trembling.

"Wanda and that Lauren gal explained what was going on. Guess you kind of got blindsided."

"I thought I was done with Payne Dearborn." A shudder worked its way up her spine. "I never expected...*this.*"

Kent didn't speak for so long that Erin grew uncomfortable. She slid a nervous glance his way and read all kinds of questions behind his narrowed eyes.

"I'm trying to understand," he said. "I get why you want to leave the past in the past. But are you saying you never reported what this guy did to you?"

"I had Avery to think about." Erin crossed her arms and stared out the windshield. "You weren't there. You don't know how it was."

Kent twisted sideways in the seat. Freeing Erin's right hand, he held it tenderly. "Then tell me."

Grief and guilt surged upward through her chest. She choked back a sob. "I don't know if I can."

"Take your time. I'm not going anywhere."

Calm strength spread from his hand to hers, until at last the words began to flow. "At first, I didn't realize what was happening, and I certainly wouldn't have labeled it abuse. Payne was under so much stress at the hospital, so sometimes he drank a little more than usual. And when he got drunk, he'd say things I knew he couldn't possibly mean."

"Say things. Like what?"

"Words I'd never allow to pass my lips." Erin winced, recalling the vile names he'd called her, the cruelly cutting remarks that disparaged her. "But by the time he sobered up, it was like he didn't even remember saying those things. Maybe you won't believe this, but I really did love him, and I believed he loved me."

"Love doesn't intentionally inflict harm—verbal or physical."

Erin nodded. "I know that now."

After giving her a few moments to sniff back tears, Kent asked quietly, "How long before he started hitting you?"

"It was our second wedding anniversary, and I'd just told him I was pregnant." The memory still felt so raw, slashing Erin's heart like a hot knife. "I thought he'd be thrilled, but instead he was furious I'd let it happen when he'd just partnered with another doctor in private practice."

Kent's fingers tightened around hers, his anger palpable. "Tell me, Erin. Tell me what he did to you."

"It actually wasn't that bad." She released a harsh laugh. "At least, I didn't think so at the time. He just grabbed my arm and twisted. It was over so quickly that I thought it was a fluke. The next morning, when I showed him the bruise, he apologized like crazy and promised it would never happen again."

Kent looked away with a snort.

"He did try, and things were okay for a while." After all that she'd been through, Erin couldn't explain why she was defending Payne now. Maybe she needed to believe her nine years with the man hadn't been utterly irredeemable.

With Kent's urging and another handful of tissues, she continued the story. After Payne's initial outrage, he'd made what seemed a genuine effort to support her during the pregnancy. Over the next few months, he drank less and appeared to truly embrace the idea of becoming a father. After Avery was born, nearly a year went by without one of Payne's explosions, and Erin got her hopes up that fatherhood had softened him.

But as the years passed, the peaceful times grew shorter and his abusive eruptions more cruel. He was good at finding ways to hurt her that didn't show. He'd also mastered how to crush her self-confidence with a perfectly timed barb, then turn around and make her believe he loved her and couldn't live without her. She'd been on an endless emotional seesaw as she struggled to anticipate his moods while keeping Avery out of the line of fire.

"What about your parents?" Kent asked. "Didn't they have a clue what was happening?"

"My father passed away before I finished high school. Mom died the year before I met Payne. I didn't have anyone but my brothers. Shaun's a missionary so he wasn't even around to know. And I didn't dare risk what Greg would do if he so much as suspected Payne was hurting me." Glancing away, Erin gave a rueful sigh. "If I'd trusted him more when I finally found the courage to leave Payne, things might be a lot different now."

"What are you saying?"

"I was so ashamed of my stupidity that I couldn't admit to my family why I really wanted out of my marriage." With a tired sigh, Erin confessed that today wasn't the first time she'd met Lauren Hall. The woman was a pharmaceutical rep who often stopped in at Payne's clinic, and their business relationship eventually led to an affair. Erin had claimed Payne's infidelity as grounds for the divorce, and Greg had helped her find an attorney.

"Greg knows now about the abuse, doesn't he?"

"He had his suspicions, and I eventually admitted the truth." Erin twisted the tissue in her lap. "You have to understand. Back then, all I wanted was an end to things, and Payne told me privately that no one would believe me anyway. If I didn't bring up the abuse in court and agreed to a minimal settlement for child support, he'd let me go and I'd never have to see or hear from him again."

"Erin…" Kent's disappointed frown made her look away.

"I know what you're going to say—that my silence enabled Payne to hurt another woman. I will never be able to forgive myself for what Lauren has suffered at Payne's hands." Throat aching, lips pressed together, she gazed toward the rocky juniper-covered hills. "But to dredge up my own past, to risk drawing my daughter into the middle of all this? I can't do it. I just can't do it."

Remaining calm and supportive while listening to Erin describe her abusive marriage and the aftermath required every last ounce of Kent's willpower. He didn't know how much longer he could keep the lid bolted down on the cauldron of fury boiling through his gut, all of it directed at the source of Erin's torment. Either Erin deserved an Academy Award for hiding the truth for so long, or her friends and family were all total idiots for not noticing how Payne was hurting her. Serving in Afghanistan, Kent had seen too many men and women in pain. Even when they'd tried to put up a front, the signs were always there. A subtle tightening around the lips and eyes, stiff posture, the avoidance of physical touch.

And the emotional wounds? Those were sometimes even more obvious. Kent had seen battle-toughened marines so tortured by PTSD that they spent every waking minute on hyperalert. Fear made it crucial to assess every room they entered and maintain a direct line of sight to all doors and windows. Kent himself startled at any sound resembling gunfire or the scream of an incoming mortar. And relationships? Too risky. A sudden flashback could mean inadvertently hurting a loved one—another reason Kent had held himself aloof all these years.

But he also understood that sometimes even the best of friends pretended not to notice the outward signs of trauma. Whether doubting their suspicions, or unwilling to cause embarrassment, or simply having no clue how to help, people had all kinds of reasons for staying silent. He'd seen it happen among fellow sailors and marines, and he'd experienced it with his own struggles after leaving the service.

So he couldn't blame Erin, and he couldn't blame her friends and family. But, just as his talks with Pastor Terry were helping him come to terms with his own emotional scars, he knew Erin had to face up to what happened or she'd never be free.

"Erin," he said, reclaiming her hand, "you are so much stronger than you realize. And so is Avery. Could you really live with yourself if you let Payne off the hook this time?"

Lips trembling, she shook her head. "I—I don't know. I have to think."

Kent checked his watch. "Avery gets out of school at three fifteen, right? Let me drive you home so you can pull yourself together before you pick her up. I'll get somebody to bring me back later for my truck."

When she agreed, he jogged back to lock the pickup while she moved over to the passenger seat. Returning to Erin's car, he climbed in behind the wheel and turned the car around to head back toward Juniper Bluff. A few minutes later, he parked in Erin's driveway.

"You don't have to stay with me," she said as he walked her to the front door.

Arms resting on her shoulders, he looked her square in the eye and gave her his most compelling smile. "What if I want to?"

A big wet tear pooled at the corner of her nose. "Thank you."

He took the key from her hand and unlocked the door. "Go freshen up. I'll make you some tea."

She didn't ask where he learned how to brew a cup of tea, and he didn't explain he was just winging it. But tea sounded like something that would help, and he was all about helping Erin get through this.

An electric kettle sat next to the stove. Kent added water and hit the start button. While the water heated, he remembered seeing a canister of Lady Grey in the cupboard the day he'd repaired her broken shelf. Next to the canister, he found a pretty ceramic mug emblazoned with curly script. *All I need is more tea and more Jesus.*

Yep, that sounded like Erin.

She stepped up next to him as he poured water over a tea bag. "You found my favorite tea and mug."

"I'm quite the industrious cowboy, in case you haven't noticed." He dunked the tea bag a couple of times. "Didn't know if you use sugar, though."

"I'm a honey girl, actually." She reached past him for the squeeze bottle sitting in the cupboard and added a dollop to her tea. Tilting her head, she beamed a grateful smile. "If you hadn't come for me, I don't know what I would have done."

He longed to stroke her freshly washed cheek and kiss away the remnants of her tears. "You'd have found your way back," he said, meaning more than simply her route home. "But I'm glad I could be there for you." *I always want to be there for you.*

The thought settled deep in Kent's chest, warming him as surely as the cup of tea soothed and comforted Erin. This talented, brave, beautiful woman had come to mean more to him than he'd ever dreamed possible.

"Kent, what is it?" Erin looked up at him with worry in her gaze.

He gave his addled brain a quick shake. "Nothing, just thinking."

"I've totally ruined your day." She was about to start crying again. "Kent, I'm so—"

He shot her a warning glare. Stepping closer, he relieved her of the mug and set it on the table, then cupped her face with both his hands. Looking into her blue eyes shimmering with unshed tears, he could hardly force the words from his throat. "There is nothing you could ever say or do that would ruin my day. You're like a fresh breeze blowing through my life, and every moment I spend with you brings nothing but the greatest kind of happiness."

"Kent—"

He kissed her then, sweetly and tenderly. Drawing away, he murmured, "That wasn't meant as an expectation or an assumption. It was my promise as a man who would never hurt you. A man who wants with all his heart to make you happy."

She slid her arms around him and nestled against his chest. "Even if I can't find it within myself to testify against Payne?"

"Even if," he said, brushing his lips across the top of her head. "But even though I haven't known you very long, I know the kind of woman you are. And I know you'll do what's right."

When it came time for Erin to pick up Avery from school, Kent asked her to drop him off at Diana's Donuts. He figured one of the regulars wouldn't mind giving him a lift out to his pickup. Besides, after the emotion-packed afternoon he'd just had, strong coffee and a sugary doughnut sounded like the ideal comfort food.

"Hey, stranger," Diana greeted as he stepped up to the counter. "I passed your house the other day on the way out to visit my folks. It's nice to see the old Gilliam homestead looking so good again."

"Been putting it off too long." Kent asked for a black coffee and the last two crullers in Diana's display case. "Erin's helping me redo the inside—sooner than I'd planned on, actually." He explained about the sesquicentennial and his correspondence with Nelson Gilliam's daughter. "I'm hoping it'll live up to the old man's memories."

"What a sweet thing for you to do, Kent." Diana smiled warmly as she handed him his change. "And I'm glad you're spending more time with Erin—though it's amazing she has a spare moment these days. More than a few of my customers have mentioned calling on her for redecorating help."

"Word's spread fast since she's been working at Wanda's." Kent's thoughts returned to Erin's encounter with Lauren Hall, and his belly tightened. He glanced around the café, wondering if the woman had stayed in town in hopes of changing Erin's mind.

He didn't see Lauren, but he did notice Pastor Terry and his wife at a corner table. With a nod to Diana, he took his coffee and crullers and ambled over. "Hi, Pastor. Excuse me for interrupting."

"Kent, good to see you. Have you met my wife, Gwen?"

"Not officially." Kent accepted her handshake. "My pleasure. I wonder if I might borrow your husband for a quick word."

Gwen Ulbright stood and picked up her mug. "Take my seat. I was just about to ask Diana for a refill."

As Kent slid into the chair, Pastor Terry said, "I can see something's troubling you. What's on your mind?"

"I don't want to break a confidence, but could you say some extra prayers for a friend who's facing a tough decision?"

Pastor Terry nodded. "Of course. Actually, I'm glad we ran into each other. You've been in my thoughts and prayers since our last meeting, and this morning it felt like the Lord pointed me to a Bible verse I should share with you." The pastor pulled his cell phone from his pocket. "Mind if I send it to you in a text?"

"That'd be fine." Kent waited while the pastor pushed some buttons on his phone. A minute later, Kent's phone chimed with the incoming text signal.

"You can read it later," Pastor Terry said as his wife returned to the table. "Think on it and we'll talk more next time we meet. I think we're still on for Friday afternoon?"

"Right. See you then." Thanking the pastor, Kent carried his coffee and crullers to an empty table.

Curious about the scripture passage, Kent opened the text. The verse was from Isaiah.

When thou passest through the waters, I will be with thee; and through the rivers, they shall not overflow thee: when thou walkest through the fire, thou shalt not be burned; neither shall the flame kindle upon thee.

One word repeatedly jumped out at him—*through*. With all the trials the writer addressed, there was no suggestion of attempting to alter difficult circumstances, no mention of circumventing the problem, no hint of turning tail and running far, far away. The passage read like a clear assumption that troubles were bound to come, but with firm assurance that God would always be there to give strength, courage and protection.

The words grabbed hold of Kent like something—no, more like *Someone*—real and alive and powerful. Like the hand of God burrowing into his chest and wrapping around his heart, not to crush it like one of those fairy-tale villains on TV, but with the gently protective care of a loving Father.

He was glad he had his back to most of the other patrons, because otherwise they were about to see a grown man cry. Leaving his coffee and crullers untouched, he eased away from the table and silently slipped out. With his hat jammed low on his forehead, he took a few steps down the block before remembering he'd left his pickup several miles south of town.

Great. *Way to make a graceful exit, Ritter.*

While he pondered his next move, a silver sedan pulled into an empty parking space in front of him. Lauren Hall stepped from the car, drawing to an abrupt halt as she recognized Kent. The hair and makeup that had been model perfect this morning looked bedraggled now. She must be as emotionally whiplashed as Kent felt at the moment, though he doubted either one of them could compare with what Erin was going through.

Going through. Those words would forever hold new meaning for him.

He breathed in slowly before offering a concerned smile. "Wondered if you'd stuck around."

"I was planning to stay for as long as it took to convince Erin to testify, but…" A trembling sigh escaped. "It seems unlikely she'll change her mind, so I was going to grab some coffee before I head back to Dallas."

Kent massaged his jaw. "Is there a trial date?"

"The first Monday of June."

A month away. Kent didn't want to give Lauren false assurance, but he also couldn't let her leave with no hope at all. "Does Erin know how to reach you?"

Lauren's lips flattened. "We never got that far."

He pulled out his cell phone. With his contacts app opened, he passed the phone to Lauren. "Give me your info. I'll keep talking to Erin."

"You'd do that?" Doubt creased her forehead. "But you don't even know me."

"I know Erin."

Eyes filling, she smiled her thanks, then thumb typed her contact information. Finishing, she pressed the phone into Kent's hand. "Please, when you see Erin, tell her again how sorry I am for bringing all this up for her. I'd never have asked if I thought there was any other way."

"She knows." Kent tucked the phone into his pocket, then tipped his hat. "Have a safe trip home."

As Lauren hurried into Diana's Donuts, Kent started down the sidewalk, only to be reminded once more that his pickup was still miles away.

Chapter Twelve

I know you'll do what's right.

No matter how hard Erin tried to ignore Kent's parting words from Wednesday, over the next couple of days they whispered through her thoughts again and again.

She also hadn't stopped reliving the kiss. With Payne's kisses, there had typically been an undercurrent of possessiveness, which at first had flattered her—until she came to understand what belonging to Payne Dearborn entailed.

But Kent's kiss had made her feel treasured. Appreciated. Respected. There hadn't been the slightest indication that he expected more. This was a new experience for Erin, and she was still pondering what it meant—what she dared *allow* it to mean for her future.

Kent telephoned Thursday and again on Friday, little more than a quick "How are you doing?" and to remind her he'd be around if she felt like talking or needed anything. She might have done well to accept his offer but preferred to get a better grip on her emotions first—and not merely those involving her encounter with Lauren Hall.

What with working at the gift shop, visiting a customer's home to consult about a bedroom makeover and sewing Kent's curtains, the time went quickly. By the weekend, she had Kent's kitchen curtains ready to hang, and with Avery pestering her about visiting the new calf, she couldn't keep putting off a trip out to the ranch. She phoned Kent Saturday morning to arrange a time.

"I'm here all day," he said. "Maybe after Avery visits with Prince, we could pack a picnic and saddle up some horses."

Erin wasn't so sure about the horseback ride, but Avery would be thrilled. "How about I bring lunch? I have fixings on hand for chicken salad."

"That's an offer I won't refuse. See you in an hour or so?"

"Sounds good." Thoughts bouncing back to his previous remark, she chuckled. "You're really calling the calf Prince?"

"Figured it suited the spoiled-rotten little critter. Y'all won't believe how much he's grown in a week."

Arriving at the ranch later, Erin had to agree. The calf looked healthy and happy—and definitely spoiled. He practically begged for Avery to come into the stall and pet him, and Kent had to run interference to keep the little guy from knocking Avery over.

"Can I help give him a bottle of milk?" Avery asked as she snuggled the calf's neck.

"He's only eating twice a day now," Kent explained, "and he's already had breakfast."

"Then how about supper? Can I feed him his supper?"

Glancing at Kent, Erin chewed her lip. "Honey, I don't think we can stay that long."

"Let's play it by ear, okay?" Kent allowed Avery a

few more minutes with the calf and then invited them to the house.

They stopped at Erin's car for her picnic cooler and the curtains she'd brought. "I hope you like how they turned out."

"And I hope you like what I've gotten done this week." Kent wiggled his brows as he relieved her of the cooler. "The old place is looking pretty good."

It truly was, Erin observed as she stepped inside the kitchen. She set her canvas tote on the table and pulled out a curtain panel. Unfolding it, she offered one end to Kent. "Here, let's see how it's going to look."

He stepped behind the table, and together they held the panel across the window. A smile of appreciation spread across his face. "This house is looking more and more like a home every day. Let's get these curtains hung."

Kent had already mounted the hardware Erin had told him he'd need. Erin fed the fabric onto the rods, and then Kent set them in position—a valance and café curtains over the sink, a larger set for the window overlooking the breakfast table and a curtain with tiebacks for the half-glass back door.

Arms folded, Erin stood in the center of the kitchen to admire the results. "Perfect. Now you just need some homey wall decor."

Kent narrowed one eye. "You mean my Zipp's Hardware calendar isn't going to cut it?"

"Uh, no," Erin said with a smirk. She tapped a finger to her lips. "I might have a few things I haven't unpacked yet. Or we could look around Wanda's Wonders next week."

"*We* obviously means *you* will do the picking, because in case you haven't noticed, I was born without a decorator gene."

Erin laughed, and after the last few days, it felt amazingly good. "Show me what you've done with the rest of the house."

The downstairs looked pretty much done. Kent had thrown out the dingy living room drapes, which he'd probably need to replace eventually, but the white venetian blinds looked passable now that they'd been cleaned and repaired. Upstairs, Kent had finished painting the two guest rooms and had started on the master. He'd definitely need new curtains for all the bedrooms and a few pretty things for the walls and dresser tops.

"Get your measuring tape," Erin instructed, already on her way to the landing. "I'll get my notebook and then we can talk about—"

"Erin." Kent's tone grew low and insistent, his gaze intense.

She could guess what he wanted to talk about. Stomach jumping, she forced a bright smile. "Or we can wait and do it after lunch. Are you ready for the picnic?"

"I am!" Avery piped up. "Which horse do I get to ride?"

Kent's eyes shuttered briefly, a silent sigh escaping between tight lips. He sank onto his haunches to tweak Avery's ponytail. "Your choice, Posey or Petunia. They're both gentle as can be."

"Petunia's the one with the white on her face that's shaped like a flower, right?"

Kent nodded.

"I pick her." She looked up at Erin. "So, Mommy, you get Posey. Is that okay?"

"Sure, honey." She'd rather skip the horseback ride entirely, but at least this line of conversation had circumvented Kent's attempt to bring up Lauren Hall's request. She preferred not to have that discussion at all, and certainly not while Avery remained within earshot. "Shall we get going, then?"

Returning to the kitchen, she helped Kent move the food from the bulky cooler to an insulated saddlebag. He added bottled water and canned soft drinks, then tossed a rolled-up blanket across his shoulder before leading them out to the barn.

With the horses saddled and the picnic supplies secured, he found a couple of riding helmets for Erin and Avery. Erin accepted hers with a suspicious frown. "This is all I get? No safety belt? Bubble wrap? Full body armor?"

Kent's gaze warmed into an inviting grin. "If it'd make you feel safer, you're sure welcome to ride double with me."

Safer? She seriously doubted it, at least where her emotions were concerned. She drew her shoulders back. "If Avery can do this, I certainly can."

"All righty, then." Kent boosted Erin into the saddle and adjusted her stirrups, then did the same for Avery. After climbing onto Jasmine, he led the procession out of the barn and through a gate into an adjoining pasture.

Parts of the trail were familiar from Erin's first encounter with Kent, but this time she actually got to enjoy the view, especially as she began to relax into Posey's easy gait. The bluebonnets that were such a brilliant blue a month ago had faded, but now winecups, Indian paintbrush, evening primrose and other wildflowers painted the rocky, rolling land in myriad colors. The breeze carried the pungent scent of mountain cedar, along with another aroma not quite so pleasant. Erin wrinkled her nose as they rode past a few head of cattle.

Riding between her and Avery, Kent snickered. "Big-time cattle ranchers would say that's the smell of money."

"And you?" Erin asked.

After a long, thoughtful moment, he responded softly, "Contentment. The smell of a good and happy life."

She studied him as he gazed out at his herd and saw something in him that hadn't been there a month ago, at least not to this degree. Though his love for ranching and the Texas Hill Country had been obvious from their first meeting, he did seem more content, more at ease with himself…and with God?

And just when Erin's faith seemed to have hit a brick wall. Prayer had come hard the last few days, as if she couldn't guess why. The times she felt most distant from God were typically when she knew deep down she was trying to escape His will.

She certainly hadn't prayed much while dating Payne, or she might have heeded the warning tugs on her heart. Now it wasn't only Erin who had to live with the consequences of that mistake but also her innocent daughter.

And Lauren Hall and every other woman Payne Dearborn may end up hurting because you're too scared to do your part in holding him accountable.

Erin had grown quiet, and Kent could easily imagine the troubling thoughts she wrestled with. When she'd asked about coming out today, he'd hoped he could get her to talk about this thing with Lauren Hall, but all morning long she had doggedly avoided any mention of the case against her ex.

Up ahead stood the spreading oak where Kent had first found Erin on his property. She'd definitely chosen an ideal spot to lay out a quilt and enjoy a spring day. He motioned toward the tree. "How about we have our picnic here?"

Erin's blue eyes, shaded by the helmet brim, softened in a smile. "Perfect."

"This is where I met your mom," Kent told Avery. "Right under that tree. She was making your birthday basket."

"Really?" Avery rose in her stirrups for a better view of the tree and the hillside sloping down to the creek. "It's so pretty. I wish I could have a tree house and come out here to play every day."

"A tree house, eh? Why didn't I think of that?" Kent chuckled as he climbed down from Jasmine and gathered up Petunia's reins. "This is a long way from the house, though. You'd have to ride a horse out here to play."

"I would love that!"

"But not by yourself, young lady," Erin stated. "At least until you're older—and maybe not even then."

Realizing what this conversation implied, Kent exchanged a nervous glance with Erin. A coral blush rose in her cheeks as heat singed his own face. They both quickly looked away.

"Y'all hungry? I sure am." He helped Erin and Avery dismount, then passed them the picnic supplies to set out while he secured the horses.

By the time he finished, Erin had unrolled the blanket on the grass and had started unwrapping sandwiches. "I hope you like rye bread."

"I spread the mayonnaise." Avery handed Kent a pink flowered paper plate and matching napkin.

"I'm sure you did a fine job." Kent awkwardly lowered himself onto the blanket—not easy in boots and snug jeans—and held out the plate for one of Erin's sandwiches. Whatever she used in her chicken salad recipe gave it an enticing aroma, and he almost forgot to wait for Erin to offer grace.

Then he noticed she'd already started eating. Avery had noticed, too, her eyes growing wide. "Mommy, you forgot to bless the food."

"Oops." Biting her lip, Erin set down her plate. "Would you like to pray, honey?"

With a sidelong glance at Kent, Avery whispered, "I think Mr. Ritter should."

His throat clenched. He was gradually getting better with his private conversations with the Lord, but he sure didn't feel ready for prime time. But when Avery smiled up at him, then folded her hands and bowed her head, he was trapped. "Okay, here goes. Lord, thank you for this beautiful day and for the chance to share it with two lovely ladies. Bless this food. Amen."

"Mom," Avery said with a giggle, "he called us *lovely ladies*."

Erin's sparkling eyes melted Kent's heart. "That was a very nice prayer. Thank you."

"Hoping I'll improve with practice." He cast her a meaningful grin. "I had a good teacher after all."

She replied with a tense smile and picked up her sandwich.

Kent did the same, savoring a bite of Erin's delicious chicken salad as he scooted back against the tree trunk and stretched out his legs.

With only a half sandwich, Avery finished first and asked if she could have her dessert now so she could explore. Erin opened a plastic container and handed her daughter an oatmeal cookie. Avery gobbled it down, then skipped off toward the creek—after a warning from her mom not to get too close to the water.

"She'll be fine." Kent shifted closer to help Erin pack up the remains of their lunch. "The creek's only a few inches deep."

"That's all it takes to drown."

"We won't let her out of our sight, okay?" But with Avery beyond eavesdropping range, maybe Kent could finally get Erin to talk more freely. He slid his hand across the blanket until their fingers met. "We've talked about everything today except what we both know is eating you alive. Don't you think it's about time?"

Erin drew her knees up and wrapped her arms around them, her gaze following her daughter along the creek bank. "I know it's the right thing to do. And I know I made lots of mistakes in how I dealt with my marriage. But I've gotten through it the best way I know how."

"See, that's the thing. I'm learning it's about more than just getting through a tough situation. I'm learning what really matters is Who's walking alongside us every step of the way."

"Who. You mean God?" Erin gave her head a sad shake. "It occurred to me this week that my faith isn't nearly as strong as I've made it out to be. If running into Lauren Hall can undermine my confidence so easily, what hope do I have?"

Reciting part of the verse he'd committed to memory, he murmured, "'When thou walkest through the fire, thou shalt not be burned; neither shall the flame kindle upon thee.'" He freed one of Erin's hands to cradle in his own. "That's the hope you have, Erin. We've both already been through the fire—you with your abusive marriage, and me with my service in Afghanistan. Maybe we didn't grasp it at the time, but God was always there. Look at us," he said, cupping her cheek until she met his gaze. "Today, right now, we're safe and whole. God didn't abandon us. He carried us through to the other side."

A tear slid down her cheek. When he kissed it away, she shivered and nestled against his chest. "You think I should testify, don't you?"

"I think if you don't, you'll never be able to leave Payne Dearborn in the past and get on with your life."

She didn't speak for several long moments, but he could feel her slowly relaxing into him. "I can't involve Avery, though. And I'd have to go to Dallas."

"She could stay with me. School will be out by then, and she'd have a blast here on the ranch."

Erin cocked her head to frown up at him. "What do you know about taking care of a seven-year-old?"

"Wait," he said with a smirk. "I thought *she'd* be taking care of me."

Avery chose that moment to plop down on the blanket with them. "Mom, are you going somewhere? Am I going to stay with Mr. Ritter?"

Sitting up with a start, Erin pivoted to face her daughter. "It's nothing for you to worry about, honey. This is grown-up business."

"Is it about why you've been so sad since the other day?" Avery's brows drew together in an angry frown. "Did Daddy do something else mean to you?"

Erin clutched her stomach. "No. I mean—"

"Let me try," Kent said, lightly touching Erin's arm. He pushed to his feet and reached for Avery's hand. "Let's take a walk, sweetheart."

Near the creek, a sturdy low-growing oak branch made an ideal seat. Kent eased onto the branch, then helped Avery up beside him. "I guess you're big enough to understand that not all husbands and daddies know how to treat their girls."

Avery gave a solemn nod. "Eva has a really nice daddy. I wish my daddy was like Mr. Austin. But Daddy used to hurt Mommy and say mean things to her and make her cry, and that's why we don't live with him anymore."

Kent noticed Erin had moved close enough to listen, and he cast her a reassuring smile before returning his attention to Avery. "Do you understand that when somebody hurts another person bad enough, a policeman might have to make him stop?"

Again, the little girl nodded.

"Well, after you and your mom left your daddy, he started hurting another lady, and now she wants your daddy to face the consequences. Do you know what consequences are?"

"It's like a punishment, isn't it? Like sometimes when I don't obey Mom and she sends me to my room."

Beyond Avery's line of vision, Erin smothered a teary-eyed laugh.

"Kind of like that, yes." Kent slipped an arm around Avery's shoulders. "But what happens with grown-ups is they have to go to court, and a judge needs everybody who might know something to answer lots of questions to make sure he has all the facts."

"So…my daddy has to go to court?"

"He does. And your mom needs to go, too, so she can tell the judge how your daddy hurt her."

Avery looked up, eyes wide with worry. "Will my daddy have to go to jail?"

"That's up to the judge. But the most important thing," Kent said, meeting Avery's gaze, "is that if there's a way to help your daddy become a better, nicer person, that's what the judge wants, too."

Erin drew closer, easing onto the branch next to Avery and twining her fingers with her daughter's. "I won't do this unless it's okay with you, honey, because you're more important to me than anything in all the world."

"Is Mr. Ritter right, though? Will the judge help Daddy be nicer?"

"The judge will think hard about what's right and best for all of us. But learning to be nicer is really up to your dad."

Avery drew her lips between her teeth. "Okay, then." With a sidelong glance at Kent, she stretched up to cup her mouth around Erin's ear but whispered loud enough for Kent to overhear, "I like Mr. Ritter a lot, but could I maybe stay with Eva instead? She has more fun stuff to play with at her house."

"What?" Kent drew back, hand over his heart like he'd been stabbed. "You'd pick Eva's toys and games over helping me take care of Prince?" At Avery's look of chagrin, he patted her knee. "I'm kidding, sweetie. It's fine."

"We have a few weeks to figure all this out," Erin said, "but thank you, honey, for being so understanding." Eyes shining, she smiled up at Kent and added softly, "And thank *you*."

Chapter Thirteen

The thought of testifying against Payne tied Erin's stomach in knots, but with the decision made, she felt freer than she had in years. After she took Avery to school on Monday, she opened her phone to the contact information Kent had given her for Lauren. Leave it to him to believe in Erin even when she doubted herself.

"I've had a change of heart," she said when Lauren answered. "Tell me what you need me to do."

"Erin, thank you." Lauren could barely choke out the words, and it took her a moment to continue. She explained the prosecuting attorney would be in touch to interview Erin and provide more details about the trial. "I know you have your daughter to think about. Will it be a problem for you to come to Dallas?"

"I have friends and family here who will help. And Avery's been amazing about the whole thing." Remembering Kent's gentleness as he took Avery aside after their picnic, Erin smiled. Did the man have any idea he was her hero? Someday, she'd have to tell him so.

"It's good you're not alone." The regret shading Lauren's tone suggested she didn't have a support system, which made Erin all the more sorry she hadn't taken advantage of her own when her marriage began to sour.

"Lauren, please forgive me for how I responded at first. If you ever feel the need to talk—about Payne or anything at all—I'm here." After a moment's hesitation, Erin added, "And I'll be praying, for both of us."

They ended the call with Lauren saying the attorney would telephone Erin in the next few days. Since the case against Payne and everything else in Erin's life truly was in God's hands, she made a conscious effort to focus on the present—which today included another trip to Fredericksburg to select fabric for Kent's bedroom curtains.

Insisting on keeping things as undemanding for Erin as possible, Kent said he'd install new window shades in each bedroom. Erin would only need to create color-coordinated valances for the guest rooms. For the master bedroom, though, she envisioned something more elegant, sheer floor-length panels accented with a damask valance and side panels with tiebacks.

She did her measuring, cutting and sewing in the evenings while Avery read aloud from a library book or completed her arithmetic and spelling homework. Wanda asked about her progress almost every day and continued her good-natured arm-twisting about forming a partnership. Erin had to admit, the idea was growing on her. "Maybe once the trial is over," she hedged. "I'll be able to think more clearly then."

On Thursday afternoon, the prosecuting attorney, Raymond Poulter, called. Asking first if he could record the conversation, he spent nearly two hours grilling Erin about her relationship with Payne. The most difficult question to answer was why she'd never told anyone.

Who could possibly understand how desperately she wanted to believe it wasn't as bad as it seemed, how hard she had worked to explain it all away, either as Payne's job stress or her own misinterpretation of events?

Ending the call, Erin sank deep into the sofa cushions and laid her head back. After spending the last several months trying to forget, and now being forced to relive it all, she was exhausted. Had agreeing to testify been a huge mistake?

No, Kent was right. Whatever the outcome of the trial, confronting Payne and his abuse was the only way she'd ever truly be free of him. She needed to lean upon God's strength more deeply than ever and to trust Him to see her through to the end.

By Saturday, Erin had finished Kent's curtains and called to ask about bringing them out.

"Doc Ingram's here this morning helping me vaccinate some cows," he said. "I'll be around this afternoon, though."

"Great. I'll see you then." Conveniently, Avery had been invited to a classmate's birthday party beginning at one o'clock, and having only spoken to Kent on the phone all week, Erin could barely suppress her eagerness to spend a little alone time with him.

Turning into his driveway shortly after dropping Avery at the party, she glimpsed him striding out of the barn, his smile warm and welcoming. He took her hand as she stepped from the car. "Thought you'd never get here."

"I've missed you, too. This week has been intense." She melted into the comfort and security of his arms.

Tilting his head, Kent brushed a wisp of hair off her face. "Did something else happen?"

"No, I'm just tired. I haven't slept well all week—even worse after those two hours on the phone with the attorney."

He dropped a kiss on the top of her head. "You can do this, Erin. Hang in there."

With a brisk nod and a shaky laugh, she pulled away. "Let's not talk about it, okay? I'd rather hang curtains."

Kent huffed. "My home improvement project is the last thing you should be worrying about right now."

"Are you kidding? It's helping to keep me from totally losing my mind." Erin reached into the back seat for the canvas tote containing Kent's curtains, and they started toward the house.

Skip offered a lazy greeting as they entered the kitchen, then traipsed after them upstairs. In the first of the guest rooms, Erin began unfolding curtains. With Kent's help, she threaded the sky blue gingham valance onto the rod.

When he set the valance in place over the window, she stepped to the center of the room to admire the results. "I love it. Not too frilly, and the checks are subtle enough not to clash with the rest of the decor."

Kent smirked. "Still a ways to go on the *decor* thing. Not much in these guest rooms besides secondhand furniture."

"Baby steps. We'll get there." Erin gathered up the remaining curtains and started for the next room.

After putting up a pale lavender valance in the mauve guest room, they moved on to the master. Erin took her time arranging cream-colored sheers and the mossy green tailored valance, then tied back the matching side panels with cords that reminded her of a cowboy's lariat. She'd even found brass Texas star ornaments to attach to the ends of the tiebacks. The overall result reflected Kent's masculinity while giving the room a touch of class.

Both of them facing the window, Kent slid an arm around Erin's waist. "Have I told you lately how amazing you are?"

"You've done the hardest work. I can't believe how quickly you got the painting done."

"None of it would have happened without you."

She stepped to the window to adjust a fold in one of the sheers. "We still need to add those finishing touches we talked about. I meant to bring a few of my extra decorative pieces, but with everything else on my mind—"

"Like you said, baby steps. We've got another three weeks or so before Mrs. Thompson brings her dad."

And three weeks before Erin's trip to Dallas for the trial. Erin closed her eyes and suppressed a nervous shudder.

Kent came up behind her, the warmth of his arms enfolding her evoking an entirely different response. "There is something else I could use your advice about. Come outside with me."

Taking her hand, he led her downstairs and out the front door. They took several steps across the lawn before he turned to face the house. He tugged something from his shirt pocket and handed it to Erin. It was the old photo Mrs. Thompson had sent.

"See?" Kent frowned. "Something's missing."

Erin looked from the house to the photo and back again. "Landscaping. We're missing shrubs and flowers."

"In case you were wondering, I'm a hundred times better at decor than I am at gardening."

Laughter erupted from Erin's belly, the first she'd experienced in days, and it felt good. "Kent Ritter, what am I going to do with you?"

His eyes darkened in a way that made her mouth go dry. He cleared his throat and faced forward again. "Thing is, with what I paid toward that bull, plus what I've already spent on paint and curtains and such, there's not much left in the budget for plants—even if I did have a clue what to do with them."

"I'm not an expert gardener by any means." Erin strove for a measure of composure. "But if we clean out the existing beds and trim up the shaggy shrubbery that's already here, then we could add a few strategically placed low-maintenance plants for now. In fact, I remember passing a discount nursery when I was in Fredericksburg the other day."

"Think you could spare some time next week to go look around with me?"

"Any chance you could break free on Tuesday? That works for me, too. Wanda gave—no, actually, she *pressured* me to take the morning off so I can meet with another interior decorating client, but I should be free by ten."

Kent gave a low whistle. "This interior design stuff is really taking off for you. I'm glad."

"It's been a blessing." Erin checked her watch—almost three thirty. She didn't have to pick up Avery for another hour. "We could do a little weeding and trimming now if you want."

"Might as well." Kent jogged to the barn to gather what gardening tools he could find.

Which turned out to be a broken-handled hoe that looked as ancient as the house, a rake missing some teeth and a pair of rusty hedge clippers. He did scrounge up a pair of work gloves Erin could wear. He'd also found an old throw rug she could kneel on so she wouldn't get her jeans too dirty.

They started on the bed nearest the front porch steps, falling into a comfortable rhythm as Kent loosened the weeds with the hoe and Erin yanked them out to toss into a rapidly growing pile.

"So this trip to Dallas," Kent began, his tone low and hesitant. "Where will you stay?"

Erin sat back on her heels and stretched. "I've been thinking about that. For obvious reasons, while I was married to Payne, I avoided letting anyone get too close. But there was one friend I'm pretty sure caught on to what was happening. I might ask if I can stay with her."

"That'd be a load off my mind. I'm starting to worry about you making the trip all by yourself."

"I'll be fine." Erin spoke with more confidence than she felt. With a fierce yank, she wrenched another weed from the bed.

Kent leaned the hoe against the house, then whipped off his hat and used a kerchief to mop the perspiration from his face and neck. He sank onto the rug next to Erin but facing the opposite direction. "Don't pretend with me, Erin. I know you're scared, and nobody on earth could blame you."

"You know what scares me most? That nothing I say will make a difference and Payne's lawyers will convince the court he's completely innocent." Shifting onto her hip, she tugged off the gloves and slapped them against her jeans. "The prosecuting attorney asked me to try to come up with anything that would corroborate my testimony, but I've got nothing. Even my medical records would be too sketchy to be convincing."

"This friend, though—you said she might have suspected?"

"Yes. Her name's Carla Perez. I was taking basketry lessons from her." Erin clenched her jaw and glanced away. "Until Payne put a stop to it."

She'd never forget Carla's disbelieving stare, then the flash of anger the day Erin had told her she wouldn't be coming back. Erin had berated herself for delivering the message in person, but she'd wanted to complete that one last basket Carla had been helping her with. Then her sleeve had slipped up, revealing the palm-shaped bruise on her forearm, and though she'd quickly tugged the sleeve down, Carla had noticed.

Now, if Carla could still describe what she'd seen that day, she could well serve as the corroboration Raymond Poulter was hoping for.

If only it proved to be enough.

Kent felt better knowing Erin might have a friend to stay with, especially someone who was aware of the abuse and could offer support as Erin testified. They worked a little longer in the flower beds, until Erin said she needed to pick up Avery. They detoured through the house for a cold drink before Kent walked her out to her car.

"Let me know what your friend says, okay?"

"I'll call her this evening. See you in church tomorrow?"

"Count on it." Kent used his thumb to brush a fleck of garden dirt from just below her ear. It felt so natural to weave his hand through the auburn wisps at her nape and pull her close for a kiss.

"I—I've got to go," she murmured, pulling away with a shaky smile. She slid behind the wheel and moments later drove away.

Kent spent the remainder of the afternoon pulling weeds and clipping deadwood from the overgrown shrubs. Even the small amount of work they'd done had made a noticeable difference. The better the house looked, the more enthusiastic Kent had grown for this project.

Or maybe he just enjoyed spending time with Erin.

On Sunday morning, he found her with Avery in their usual pew, with a seat saved just for him. This was starting to feel natural, too, and Kent didn't know which amazed him more—that he was attending church again, or that he'd begun to envision a future where Erin and her daughter were a permanent part of his life.

Apparently, he should have paid closer attention to the calendar, though. When ushers handed out long-stemmed carnations to all the moms after church, Kent could kick himself for forgetting it was Mother's Day. He'd call his own mother later, but in the meantime, he offered to treat Erin and Avery to lunch at Casa Luis.

Over tacos and cheesy enchiladas, Erin said her friend Carla would be delighted to have Erin stay with her. She'd also arranged for Avery to stay with the Austin family, which left Kent feeling slightly disappointed but also relieved. If fatherhood really was a growing possibility, he could use a little more supervised practice.

On Tuesday morning after Erin's appointment, Kent picked her up for the drive over to Fredericksburg. She directed him to the discount nursery she'd mentioned, and with the help of a knowledgeable salesperson, they selected two nice-size mountain laurels for either side of the front steps. Erin suggested they also pick up a few flats of periwinkles and marigolds to add more color and greenery around the house.

They were back in Juniper Bluff by noon, and Erin invited Kent in for a sandwich before following him out to his place to start planting. By the time she had to leave to get Avery from school, they'd set the shrubs in place and started on the bedding plants.

"Think you can finish the rest on your own?" Erin asked as she dusted off her jeans.

Kent scoffed. "How hard can it be?"

Erin's scrunched-up nose was a clear judgment of his haphazard efforts. "Just don't plant the flowers too close together. And remember to water lightly after you're done."

"I was in the service, remember? I know how to follow orders."

"I do know," she said with a sad smile. "I hope someday you'll be ready to tell me about it."

Touché. Guess Kent couldn't blame her, considering how he'd encouraged her to talk about her difficult past. "Pastor Terry's still helping me work through some things."

"Then don't forget the verse from Isaiah you gave me." Erin's face shone with inner strength as she lightly touched his arm. "I've learned the hard way that life seems a lot less overwhelming when I share the tough times with both God and the people I care for."

"Erin, I think I…" A knot of emotion closed Kent's throat. *I'm falling in love with you*, he wanted to say, but the words wouldn't come.

Soon, though. Erin needed to get past the trial, and Kent needed to fully admit that this life of suspended animation he'd settled into, no matter how he whitewashed it as his cattle ranching dream come true, was really no life at all.

Chapter Fourteen

Kent had come to look forward to weekends, when Erin usually brought something special for lunch, along with a few more decorative items for the house. With Avery's watchful assistance, Erin plied her artistic talents hanging wall art or arranging pretty things on tables and dressers, and afterward Kent would saddle the horses and take his girls for another trail ride and picnic.

His girls. More and more, he'd begun thinking of them that way, and he liked how it made him feel.

The next couple of weeks flew by, at least for him. The hardware store plus looking after his herd and the spring calves kept him busy enough. Then the historical preservation folks called to schedule their inspection tour. If Erin hadn't been by his side that day, he'd have been a nervous wreck. But all had gone well, and with his place officially designated a historical site and a huge property tax cut on the horizon, he took out a short-term loan from the bank so he could conclude the purchase of his new bull. Two days later, he drove over to Kerrville to pick him up.

Now he just had to gear up for the visit from Mrs.

Thompson and her dad. So far, at least, he'd killed only a few of the bedding plants—most likely from over-watering, Erin had informed him. The mountain laurels beside the front steps already displayed new growth, and the nurseryman had promised fragrant purple blossoms next February or March.

For Memorial Day, the church had organized a community barbecue, with families asked to bring side dishes and desserts to share. The crowd made Kent more than a little uneasy, but he wouldn't disappoint Erin. Besides, she'd promised to bake another blueberry pie.

He arrived at Erin's around four that afternoon to pick them up for the barbecue. One look at her in white capris and an aqua ruffled tank top, and he was a goner. He whistled under his breath. "You look great."

"Thanks, cowboy." Grinning, Erin eyed him up and down. "You do realize normal guys typically wear shorts and sandals in the summertime. How can you stand wearing jeans and boots all the time?"

"Are you kidding? This is ranching country. If I showed up in shorts, I'd be laughed out of town."

Erin rolled her eyes. "Whatever." Leaving Kent standing in the entryway, she marched to the kitchen and returned a moment later with a pie container. She called down the hall to Avery, "Mr. Ritter's here, honey. Let's go."

The "Mr. Ritter" thing was starting to get to him, especially when he hoped for so much more from this relationship. "Would you have a problem if she just called me Kent?"

Head tilted, Erin offered him a thoughtful smile. "I guess not. But I've tried to teach Avery to respect her elders, and I didn't know how you'd feel about her using your given name."

"Elders?" Kent winced. "Now you're making me feel *really* old. Maybe I should have brought my cane."

Erin's laughter sparkled like the summer sunshine. "Come on, you old geezer. Let's go to the barbecue."

On the way, she explained to Avery that since Kent was now their very good friend, it was okay to use his first name.

He caught the little girl's curious grin in the rearview mirror. "I'm glad, Mom," Avery said. "Does that mean you can start calling him names like *honey* and *sweetie* like Eva's mom uses for Mr. Austin?"

Kent and Erin shared an awkward glance. "I can think of worse things you could call me," he murmured. "But either of those works fine."

"I'll keep that in mind."

The church parking lot was already filling up by the time they pulled in. Kent had purchased three canvas camp chairs for the occasion, and hefted those from the pickup bed while Erin helped Avery out of the back seat and retrieved the pie container.

"There's Eva." Avery pointed as they wove through the picnic area. "Can we sit with them?" Without waiting for an answer, she ran over to her friend.

"Hey, y'all." Christina Austin shifted the baby in her lap to wave. "Come on over."

Seth got up to help Kent set up his chairs, then widened the circle to make more room. "The Willoughbys will be joining us, too. There's cold drinks over at the food tent."

"I'll bring us something back after I drop off my pie," Erin said.

While Erin made her way to the food tent, Kent settled into the chair next to Seth, also in jeans and boots, and suppressed a smile of vindication. "How old are your twins now?"

"A little over four months." Seth beamed with pride. "That's Jacob on the quilt, and Christina's holding Elisabeth."

Motioning toward a group of boys tossing a football, Kent asked, "That's your other son over there, isn't it?"

"Yeah, Joseph's the tall, skinny towhead."

Kent nodded slowly, a twinge of envy squeezing his chest. "Fine family."

"I've been blessed, that's for sure." Grinning, Seth gestured toward the food tent, where Erin chatted with Wanda from the gift shop. "Looks like you might have a ready-made family in your future."

A month ago, Kent would have vehemently denied the possibility. Today, though…he couldn't think of anything he'd like more.

Erin returned shortly with two cups of lemonade. She took the chair on Kent's other side and struck up a conversation with Christina and Mrs. Peterson, Seth's grandmother. Soon, Tripp and Diana Willoughby arrived, and the circle expanded. While everyone else talked, Kent tried to smile or nod at all the right places. But he was way out of practice with socializing and couldn't seem to stop scanning his surroundings as if expecting a threat to materialize out of nowhere. It took an act of will to focus on Erin, her cheery voice and bright laughter a much-needed distraction.

Sometime later, he glanced down to see Christina's golden retriever with her chin on his thigh. Huge brown eyes gazed up at him as if the dog could see all the way to his soul.

The conversation ceased, and he felt everyone's eyes on him. Christina cast him a knowing smile. "Gracie can always tell when somebody needs a little reassurance."

Releasing a tense chuckle, Kent gave the dog a scratch behind the ears. "Probably just smells my dog, Skip."

"Maybe so," Christina said, but her expression suggested she thought otherwise.

Sad thing was, she wasn't wrong.

The squawk of a microphone set Kent's teeth on edge, his fight-or-flight reflex nearly propelling him out of his chair. Hoping no one else had noticed, he sat back and forced himself to breathe.

"Grab your plates, folks!" came a man's voice over the loudspeaker. "It's 'cue time!"

"That's Bryan, my grandfather," Seth said as he helped Christina corral the twins. "He and his pals have been smoking brisket all day, and it's gonna be melt-in-your-mouth delicious."

The aroma that had been tickling Kent's senses ever since they arrived reassured him this was just a church barbecue and he was surrounded by friends. Erin called to Avery, and the three of them fell in line to fill their plates with brisket, pinto beans, potato salad and a variety of other potluck dishes. Kent's plate was piled so high, he worried he wouldn't have room for a slice of Erin's pie.

It helped when Tripp talked him into a predessert game of horseshoes, teaming up with him against Seth and his grandfather. After Seth and Bryan trounced

Kent and Tripp in three successive games, they traipsed over to grab some dessert, and Kent had to thank Erin for setting aside a slice of her blueberry pie for him.

The sun was slipping behind the western hills as Kent finished his pie. He felt pleasantly stuffed, and much more relaxed than he'd been when they first arrived.

Then another announcement came over the speakers. "It's about that time, everybody, so turn your chairs to face the pond out back and get ready for our Memorial Day fireworks show!"

Fireworks? Kent's stomach heaved. He swallowed hard, hoping to keep his dinner down. Why hadn't he known there'd be fireworks?

Gracie whined at his feet, squeezing in as close as she could. The dog nuzzled his arm, and without thinking, he buried his fingers deep in her ruff. He dropped his head onto hers and inhaled the lemon-and-lavender scent of doggy shampoo.

"Kent?" Erin touched his shoulder. "Are you okay?"

Straightening slowly, he took deliberate breaths through his open mouth. "I, uh, need to…"

Seth stood and nudged Kent to his feet. "Come on, buddy. Let's take a walk."

They headed toward the parking lot. By the time they reached the other side of the church building, some of Kent's tension had subsided. "Sorry if I made a scene."

"You didn't." Seth leaned against a pillar. "It's the fireworks, right?"

"The rifle fire, the explosions—too many reminders." Kent glanced back toward the picnic area. "I can't ask Erin and Avery to miss the show, but…" He inhaled a shaky breath. "I can't stay."

"We can take them home afterward. You go on. Take care of yourself."

"You'll explain to Erin?"

Seth offered a grim smile. "I don't think I'll have to."

When Seth returned to say Kent needed to leave, Erin's first instinct was to rush after him, but Seth advised her not to. "Best to give him some space. Besides, you'll only make him feel worse if he thinks he spoiled the evening for you and Avery."

Erin couldn't argue. Even so, the fireworks show was already ruined for her, because all she could think about was Kent.

Later, after the Austins took her and Avery home, she had a terrible time getting her daughter to settle down enough to go to sleep. She pitied Miss Adams having to deal with a bunch of bleary-eyed first graders in the morning, but at least this was the last week of school before summer vacation.

Which meant only one more week until Payne's trial, and the thought was more than enough to keep Erin awake for half the night.

Before heading to the gift shop the next morning, she decided to stop in at the hardware store and make sure Kent was okay. She found him shelving boxes of nails, her gaze riveted by the way his biceps bunched each time he reached into the shipping crate.

Noticing her, he straightened with a start. "Hey. You surprised me."

"A good surprise, I hope." Erin edged nearer.

His half smile didn't quite convince her. He slid another box of nails onto the shelf. "Sorry about ducking out on you last night."

She narrowed one eye. "Seems like we've already had the no-apology discussion. Several times."

"Yeah, well...sometimes you can't get around it." Without making eye contact, he stooped to grab another box, then thoughtfully tested its weight. "Hope Avery had a good time."

"She did. We both did, until—" Erin bit off the rest of the statement. It would do no good to lay more guilt upon Kent's shoulders. She took another step closer. "Kent, I'm worried about you. I care, and I want to help."

"Nothing you can do. I've just gotta get thr—" His lips clamped shut, and he shoved the box onto the shelf. Exhaling slowly, he turned to her with a forced smile. "I should get busy. We've got a lot of catching up to do here after the holiday weekend."

"Oh. Right." Arms folded, Erin sidled away. "Call me when you get home later? I could come over after work and do a little more decorating."

"Thanks, but everything's looking pretty good now. Anyway, I've got a lot of other stuff on my plate this week, and you've got plenty to think about with your trip coming up." He'd already gone back to shelving nails.

Tears threatening, Erin muttered a terse goodbye and rushed out. She sat in the car for a full five minutes asking herself how one Memorial Day picnic could change things between them so drastically. Yes, she understood about the fireworks and why Kent had needed to get away. But why was he shutting her out completely? Was he embarrassed about revealing his vulnerability...or was it something else?

And how would she ever survive the remaining days before the trial without him?

* * *

Friday was the last day of school, and Erin could barely contain Avery's excitement about graduating from first grade. She thought she'd never get her wiggling daughter buttoned into the frilly pink dress she'd worn for Easter Sunday. "Stand still, honey. Oh, my, I think you've grown a whole inch since Easter."

"You're coming to my program, aren't you, Mom? I'm going to recite a poem I learned."

Erin laughed as she tied a big bow at Avery's waist. "For the millionth time, yes. I wouldn't dream of missing your program."

"And then I'm going to Eva's and we're going to have so much fun. Did you finish packing my suitcase yet?"

"I'll do it as soon as I get home from the gift shop later."

Erin still had her own packing to do, as well. Avery was so eager to spend the next few days with Eva at Serenity Hills that Erin agreed she could go home with the Austins following this afternoon's graduation program. Erin welcomed a little quiet time tonight to get her thoughts in order, and then she'd leave for Dallas first thing in the morning. She also looked forward to seeing Carla Perez again and soaking up the older woman's wisdom and reassurance before the trial began on Monday.

Avery buckled on her white patent Mary Janes. "Can Mr.—I mean Kent—can he come to my program, too?"

After Erin's disheartening encounter with Kent on Tuesday, she briefly considered asking her daughter to revert to calling him Mr. Ritter again. But then she'd have to explain why, and she didn't have the words. "I'm afraid not, sweetie. He's very busy right now."

"I wish he could, though." Slumping to the kitchen, Avery muttered, "Other daddies are coming."

"Avery Dearborn." Erin caught up with her daughter and drew her to a halt. "Honey, Kent is not your daddy. He's just a—a—" *What?* Erin wasn't sure she even knew anymore. She dropped to one knee and gripped Avery's shoulders. "I know you've grown attached to Kent, and I understand how much you miss having a dad who's good and kind and always there for you. I pray every day for that very thing. So let's just be patient, okay? And always trust that God is working out His very best for us."

Avery's half-hearted shrug and downturned lips said she didn't think much of Erin's response. By the time Erin dropped her at school, though, she was bubbling over again about the program.

The morning at the gift shop proved to be a quiet one, which didn't help Erin's fretful mood. When she'd dusted the same display shelf for the third time, Wanda yanked the feather duster from her hand. "Honey, if you really want to get the trial off your mind, come sit down and let's hammer out that partnership arrangement you keep putting me off about."

"Oh, Wanda, I'm still not sure—"

"I'm sure enough for the both of us. Already got some advice from my lawyer, so let me at least outline my ideas. You can mull them over for a few days, and when you're back in town next week, we can sign on the dotted line."

Heart swelling, Erin offered yet another silent prayer of gratitude for the amazing opportunities her new life in Juniper Bluff had offered. But would her growing self-confidence help her stand tall and unflinching when she faced Payne next week? *Dear God, give me strength!*

Her thoughts were spinning wildly when she returned home later to down a quick sandwich and finish packing. It was a good thing she had Avery's school program to bring her back to earth. She laughed and applauded as the graduating first graders performed poetry, skits and musical numbers for parents and friends. Miss Adams then handed each child a scroll tied with a red ribbon and pronounced them ready for second grade.

"And, children, I have some happy news," the teacher said. "At least it's happy news for me, and I hope it will be for you. I'm moving up to teach second grade next fall, so many of you will still be my students."

A chorus of excited cheers went up from the class, including from Avery and Eva.

"Yesss!" Christina, seated next to Erin, pumped her fists. "Seth and I have been praying the administration would grant Miss Adams's request. Eva took some convincing to attend public school, and the continuity will help so much."

"I'm sure it'll be good for Avery, too. Our move to Juniper Bluff has been an adjustment." Erin reached for her purse. "By the way, thank you again so much for taking care of Avery for me. I have some emergency numbers here in case you need them." She handed Christina a folded slip of paper.

Seth reached beneath his chair for his hat. "Eva's been bouncing off the walls waiting for this weekend. We'll all have a great time."

After saying goodbye to Miss Adams and collecting their daughters, Erin and the Austins strode out to the parking area. Erin transferred Avery's pink suitcase to the Austins' minivan, then gave her daughter a big hug and kiss. "Be very, very good and do whatever Mr. and Mrs. Austin tell you, okay?"

"I will, Mom." Avery cocked her head. "Are you going to cry?"

"Maybe a teensy bit." Erin gave a shaky laugh and brushed away the tear she'd failed to hold back. This was her first time being away from her daughter for more than a single night. Apparently, Avery was handling it much better than her mother.

"You'll be okay, Mom," Avery said in her best grown-up voice. Her tiny mouth puckered in a thoughtful frown. "Tell Daddy I'm praying to Jesus to make him be good."

Now Erin's tears flowed in earnest. "If I get the chance, I certainly will tell him, honey." She kissed her daughter again, then waved as Avery climbed in next to Eva. "I love you, baby. See you soon."

At home later, Erin almost couldn't bear the quiet. She was used to being home alone after work while Avery was at school, but this felt different, like the end of something—what, she wasn't sure. More than once, she fought the urge to call Kent and share the news about her talk with Wanda. If only he knew how badly she needed to hear his voice and to be reassured he hadn't completely cut her out of his life.

With her luggage packed and sitting by the door to the garage, she filled the rest of the afternoon with random cleaning and vacuuming. Too on edge to eat supper, she threw half her microwave entrée down the disposal. After an hour or so of mindless TV, she crawled into bed with a new mystery novel she hoped would distract her.

A few minutes after nine, her phone rang. When Kent's name flashed across the display, her heart raced. She answered with a quavery "Hello?"

"Hope I didn't wake you." He sounded as uncertain as she felt. "Couldn't let you leave for Dallas without saying goodbye."

Goodbye? Erin prayed he didn't mean it literally. "I'm trying to think of it as a mini vacation—at least until Monday." She struggled to keep her tone light. "But I'll miss being there when you show Mrs. Thompson and her dad around. You're doing such a good thing for them."

"Hope it's as helpful as Mrs. Thompson is counting on." Kent cleared his throat. "So, anyway, have a safe trip... Good night."

The call-ended tone sounded in her ear. Erin held the phone at arm's length, her emotions an eddy of doubt and confusion. He'd taken the time to call, which had to mean something... Didn't it?

He shouldn't have called. But he missed her like crazy, and he hadn't been able to stop himself.

The Memorial Day barbecue had been a wake-up call, though. A reminder that, ten years later, Kent had never completely recovered from his wartime service. Didn't he still jump every time a gunshot sounded from one of the hunting leases across the hills? Or when he heard a crack of thunder or a car backfire or a door slam too hard?

As for fireworks, he'd learned long ago that on New Year's Eve and the Fourth of July he needed to stay as far away from the festivities as he could get. He'd already talked with Pastor Terry about his Memorial Day episode, and the pastor had apologized profusely for failing to warn Kent that fireworks had been planned.

Yet, even with the pastor's assurance that this didn't have to become a major setback, Kent couldn't shake his disappointment in himself. If he could be so easily undone by something most people considered fun, how could he ever hope to be a normal husband and father? Kids loved fireworks, and families did things together. He didn't want to be the dad who made excuses to stay home alone while his wife and kids went out and embraced life.

Sure, Erin would try hard to understand. But he'd seen the pity in her eyes when she'd come by the hardware store on Tuesday, and he'd known in that moment that he couldn't saddle her with his issues. He needed to let her go—if only he could find the strength.

Sitting at his kitchen table, he opened his laptop to check his email. The first one to pop up was a lengthy message from his mom with news about the goings-on back home. He'd told his parents about needing to fix up his house for the sesquicentennial and that Mrs. Thompson's upcoming visit with her dad had shortened his timetable. He'd also mentioned "a friend" had been helping him redecorate. Good thing he hadn't let on how his feelings for Erin had grown or Mom would be after him for more details—and probably planning the rehearsal dinner for a wedding that would never happen.

He skimmed a couple of ranching e-newsletters he subscribed to, flagged an online bill to pay in the next few days and then came upon another message from Jean Thompson.

Just a note to let you know Dad and I left this morning for Texas. We're taking it slow and stopping often. I have hotel reservations for Monday night in Fredericksburg, and if it's still all right with you, we will drive over to Juniper Bluff on Tuesday. Would a 10:00 a.m. visit be convenient for you?

Kent had already requested the day off from the hardware store, so he typed a quick reply saying ten o'clock on Tuesday would be fine. Clicking the send button, he leaned back and let his gaze wander the newly redone kitchen—such a change from the day he'd received Mrs. Thompson's first letter nearly two months ago. From the sunshine-yellow walls, to the calico curtains, to the quirky twig fruit basket in the center of the table, every detail whispered Erin's name.

By Tuesday night, he just might have to move out of the house and take up residence in the barn.

Chapter Fifteen

❧

After several hours on the road, Erin was exhausted when she finally arrived at Carla's. Her friend wrapped her in a warm embrace, then sent her to the guest room for a nap. She awoke later to the aroma of Carla's home-made chicken enchiladas and found her way to the kitchen.

"Come sit down." Carla filled a glass with iced tea. "Thought you might sleep right on till tomorrow."

Still shaking off the grogginess, Erin covered a yawn. "Wish I could sleep through the next few days and wake up to find the trial is over and done with."

A scowl darkened Carla's usually smiling face. "I pray with all my heart that man gets what's coming to him." She dished out servings of enchiladas onto their plates. "The assistant DA deposed me a few days ago. I told him all about the last time I saw you, after Payne made you stop our lessons. Plus, I mentioned all the other times I suspected something wasn't right."

Erin pushed a bite of food around her plate. "Guess I wasn't as good at hiding it as I thought."

"Oh, you were good, all right. But my late husband had a mean streak, too, and I saw some of myself in you."

"Carla, I had no idea." Erin's gaze slid toward the hallway and a portrait Carla had said was taken on their thirty-fifth anniversary. Mr. Perez had died of a heart attack two years later. "But you stayed with him." It was a statement but also a question.

The woman shrugged while slowly chewing a bite of enchilada. "It was a long time ago. I didn't know I had choices. But you and I are both free now. And I am so proud of you for taking a stand against the likes of Payne Dearborn."

Erin was proud of herself, too. Proud to have found the courage to testify, and proud of discovering she actually could stand on her own two feet to support herself and her daughter.

But was she wrong to want more? To dream of sharing her life with a man as kind and good and true as Kent Ritter? "Carla… I've met someone. I think I'm in love with him."

"Oh, honey. Be careful." The older woman's gaze narrowed with chagrin. "Tell me honestly, when you first fell in love with Payne, could you have guessed what it would lead to?"

"No, not at first. I was too naive then to recognize the signs."

Carla's tight lips conveyed her doubts. "I just hope your experience with Payne taught you something."

Thoughts swirling, Erin twisted the napkin in her lap. Had she truly learned her lesson about rushing into a relationship? Yes, Kent's walk with the Lord seemed stronger every day. But was she still so terrified of being alone that she didn't dare peek behind her hero's "Mr. Perfect" mask?

* * *

On Tuesday morning, Kent awoke a full hour before the alarm. Crazy how today had him even more nervous than when the historical preservation people had come out… Maybe because Erin wasn't here to support him?

After feeding the horses and mucking out barn stalls, he saddled Jasmine and rode out to check on the herd and make sure all his calves were thriving. Back at the house, he yanked out a stray weed or two in the flower beds and swept the front and back porches. Inside, he ran the vacuum one more time for any last-minute traces of Skip's shedding.

Satisfied he had the house in good order, he got busy on himself. A few minutes after nine, clean-shaven and dressed in a crisp button-down shirt and his nicest jeans, he returned to the kitchen. In case his visitors cared for coffee, he rinsed out the coffee maker and added water and grounds to brew a fresh pot. Somewhere he'd read that the scent of baked goods made people feel more at home, but since he wasn't much into baking, he dropped a couple of slices of bread into the toaster.

The mantel clock had just struck ten o'clock when he heard a car in the driveway. Shooing Skip off the easy chair, he wadded up the ratty old dog blanket and stuffed it under the sofa. "Come on, boy, you're going outside for a while."

Skip reluctantly followed Kent out the front door, which might not have been the wisest move because the dog decided to dig himself a cool spot in the dirt behind one of the mountain laurel bushes. Well, this was a ranch, after all, not Buckingham Palace. Kent blew out a sharp breath and started across the lawn.

A tall, slender woman with silver-blond hair stepped

from the sedan. "You must be Kent. It's so good to finally meet you in person."

"You, too, ma'am. No trouble finding the place?"

"None at all. And it looks so much like my childhood memories of visiting my grandparents that I couldn't possibly miss it." She bustled around to the passenger door, where a frail gentleman struggled to get out of the car. "Slow down, Daddy. I'll help you."

Leaning heavily on a cane, Nelson Gilliam made his way around the car. He paused, throaty laughter erupting from his chest. "There's my barn. And my house. Horses and cattle, too, just like in the old days."

"Yes, Dad. We're here." Tears choked Mrs. Thompson's voice, and she cast Kent a grateful smile.

Despite being stooped with age, Mr. Gilliam wasn't a small man, but he stood even taller now, his face lighting up and a spring returning to his step. Both Kent and Mrs. Thompson had to hurry to keep up as he detoured to the barn. After he'd inspected every nook and cranny, he wanted to see the horses. Kent grabbed a handful of carrots from the barn refrigerator, then called Posey and Petunia over to the pasture gate so Mr. Gilliam could pet them and offer them treats.

When the old man seemed to be tiring, Kent invited his guests to the house. After pouring three mugs of coffee, he joined them at the kitchen table.

Mrs. Thompson took a careful sip from her mug. "Just look at him," she whispered to Kent. "He hasn't looked this bright and happy in months."

Seeing the utter contentment on Mr. Gilliam's face certainly made the effort of the past few weeks worthwhile. After the man had rested a bit and they'd finished their coffee, Kent showed them through the rest of the house. Mr. Gilliam seemed to know his way around just fine, though, each room prompting another story or two from his days growing up here.

Back in the living room, Mr. Gilliam strode to the front door and stepped onto the porch. Gingerly, he lowered himself to sit on the top porch step, then patted the spot beside him. When his daughter scooted in next to him, he tucked an arm around her shoulders. "Right here," he said, "is the very spot where I proposed to your mama. It was a summer day just like today, and when she said yes, I shouted so loud that my folks came a-runnin' to see if I'd been snakebit."

Leaning against the rail a few feet away, Kent chuckled to himself as he envisioned the scene. Then thoughts of Erin made his heart twist. Lost in regrets and what-ifs, he hardly noticed when Mrs. Thompson approached.

"I can't thank you enough for letting us come." She glanced at her father, still seated on the porch step and gazing out across the lawn. "And the house—you've truly made it into a home. It's charming."

Kent owed every bit of that charm to Erin.

Saying it was time to be on their way, Mrs. Thompson helped her father to his feet. Mr. Gilliam turned to Kent and locked his hand in a firm grip. "Jean says you served your country."

"I did, sir. Proudly."

"It takes a toll, though. Never was the same after I came home from Korea." The man beamed a smile toward his daughter. "I've thanked God every day since for my dear wife and our wonderful children, because when those dark places call to you, family brings you back."

Throat aching, Kent could only nod.

With more words of thanks, Mrs. Thompson linked her arm through her father's to help him down the steps. Kent walked with them to the car, then waved as they drove away.

Trudging to the house beneath the weight of exhaustion, he plopped down on the same step where Mr. Gilliam had been sitting minutes ago. *Right here is the very spot where I proposed to your mama.* Would Kent ever be able to say those words to a child of his own?

When those dark places call to you, family brings you back.

A dirty, wet nose under Kent's arm told him Skip had emerged from his hiding place. Love and devotion shone in those big brown eyes, and though Skip was family in the way only a beloved pet can be, Kent needed more.

He needed Erin.

Erin paced the small room where Mr. Poulter had asked her to wait in case she needed to take the stand again. During her initial round of questioning yesterday as she felt Payne's eyes on her in wordless condemnation, she'd refused to be intimidated. *I will be with thee*, God's word said. Whatever the struggle, whatever the trial, she did not go through it alone.

A light tap sounded on the door, and Carla peeked in. "I know you'll be leaving for home as soon as they release you, and I couldn't let you go without apologizing."

"Apologize? For what?"

Nudging the door closed, Carla lowered her eyes. "I was wrong to pass judgment on this new man in your life. Worse, to suggest in any way that you are incapable of making wise choices in relationships."

Erin reached for Carla's hand. "You were concerned for me as a friend. I understand."

"So you forgive me?"

Before Erin could reply, the door opened again, and Mr. Poulter's paralegal looked in. "Erin, Mr. Poulter is calling you back to the stand."

Butterflies swarming, she laid a hand over her abdomen.

"You can do this, honey." Carla gripped her wrists. "And when you're done, you put Payne Dearborn in your rearview mirror once and for all. Then go find that good man back in Juniper Bluff and make your happily-ever-after dreams come true."

Drawing Carla into a hug, Erin squeezed hard. "Thank you. I only hope it's not too late."

As Erin stepped into the witness box a few minutes later, she turned purposefully toward the defense table, her gaze locking with Payne's. Instincts formed over years of trying not to provoke his rage made it hard not to cower, but as she held firm, an amazing sense of calm washed over her. In the end, it was Payne who looked away, his shoulders slumping with defeat.

After another hour of questioning, Erin was finally excused. Lauren Hall caught her in the corridor. "Erin, thank you so much for everything you said. I know it wasn't easy."

"No, but I feel stronger and more at peace than I have in a long time." True, she'd shed many tears as she told her story on the witness stand, but they were cleansing tears, releasing all her pent-up emotions from the past. "I need to thank you for finding me and convincing me to testify."

"I know it made a difference. I'll call you as soon as we get a verdict."

As Erin strode out to her car, she realized the final outcome didn't matter nearly as much as the fact that in standing up to Payne Dearborn she'd conquered her greatest fear…and her greatest disappointment. The results were ultimately up to God.

Phoning Christina from the road, she estimated she'd arrive at Serenity Hills by 9:00 p.m. and said Avery should stay up to wait for her. She couldn't wait to wrap her little girl in a bear hug and tell her everything was going to be okay.

But there was someone else she needed to see just as badly, and the drive back to Juniper Bluff gave her plenty of time to ponder everything she wanted to say to Kent Ritter, beginning with *I'm in love with you*. The past few days had shown her how strong she really was, and she wasn't about to let this wonderful man—a truly godly man she believed loved her as much as she loved him—slip away.

Kent had driven himself half-crazy wondering how Erin's testimony was going. Figuring she'd be checking in with the Austins regularly, he gave up agonizing over whether he had any right to ask. He pushed aside the remains of his cold chili from a can and called the guest ranch.

"Christina heard from Erin about an hour ago," Seth told him. "Said she sounded real upbeat and was anxious to get home. Should be here around nine."

New worries tightened Kent's belly. "She's driving all the way back tonight?"

"Couldn't talk her out of it. Guess she had no real reason to stay another night in Dallas."

Kent thanked Seth and ended the call. A moment later, the mantel clock in the living room chimed half past seven. In an hour and a half, Erin could be turning in at the Serenity Hills gate.

Pacing in the silence of his kitchen, Kent wrestled with what to do next. Since Jean Thompson and her father had left earlier, he'd had plenty of time to think. Plenty of time to realize what a fool he'd be to give up on a future with the woman he grew to love more every day. Sure, they both had baggage. But what normal human being didn't have an old suitcase or two that still needed sorting through? And like his granddad used to say, a problem shared is a problem halved.

Decision made, he slapped his hat on his head, grabbed his keys and loped out to his truck. Fifteen minutes later, he was knocking on the Austins' back door.

Seth answered, his expression surprised at first, but then a knowing smile settled across his face. He showed Kent to the den, where the family, including Seth's grandparents but minus his infant twins, were watching a movie. "Look who's here, y'all."

Avery leaped from the sofa. "Kent!" Arms wrapped around his waist, she beamed up at him. "Did you know Mom's coming to pick me up?"

He ruffled her hair. "Mr. Austin told me. Not excited, are you?"

"The girls have been having a great time," Christina said, then added in a stage whisper, "but I think you-know-who is getting a little homesick."

If Avery missed her mom half as much as Kent did, he could relate.

Seth motioned toward the sofa. "Have a seat, if you can squeeze in. The movie should be over just about the time Erin gets here."

Wedged between Avery and Seth's son Joseph, Kent nearly melted when Avery snuggled in close, her pale red curls tickling his chin. She cupped her hand around his ear to whisper what the movie was about, and Kent tried to act interested in what was happening on the TV screen, but his attention kept drifting to the window for any sound of Erin's car in the driveway.

The movie ended a few minutes after nine o'clock, and Seth's grandparents excused themselves to head upstairs to bed. While Kent fidgeted on the sofa second-guessing his rush to be here for Erin's return, headlights flashed across the den window.

Avery hurried to peek out. "It's Mommy. She's here!" Spinning on her toes, she darted down the hall.

Kent froze. He shot a helpless look toward Seth and Christina.

"Don't wimp out now." Grinning, Seth signaled with his thumb toward the back door.

Kent hauled in a deep breath. *It's all up to You, God. Don't let me blow it.*

By the time he reached the door, Avery had already bolted out. Erin knelt on the lawn to sweep her daughter into a hug. "Wow, sweetie, did you miss me that much?"

"Not all the time, Mom. But I'm really, really, *really* glad you're home!" Avery edged back, her heart-shaped face growing serious. "Did you see Daddy? Is he going to be nicer now?"

"I saw him, yes. We just have to keep praying for

him." Erin pushed to her feet. Noticing Kent, she gave a tiny gasp. "You're here?"

Heart pounding, he started down the porch steps. He'd been working out in his head all the things he wanted to say, but as he strode toward her, every thought fled but one: to take Erin Dearborn in his arms and kiss her like crazy.

He did just that, and when the kiss ended, she gazed up at him with a teasing glint in her eyes. "I guess this means you missed me, too."

"More than you'll ever know." He swallowed hard. "Erin, I love you so much, and I'm sorry for pushing you away. Sorry for—"

"Stop. Let's not waste one more minute on apologies." Fingers twining through his hair, she pulled him close. "If you hadn't been here tonight, first thing in the morning I'd have been beating down your door. Because I'm crazy in love with you, too, Kent Ritter, and I don't intend to ever let you go."

Epilogue

One month later

Sweltering in his usual boots and jeans, Kent flipped one of the steaks he had sizzling on his backyard grill. If the summer got any hotter, he might have to break down and buy himself a pair of those Bermuda shorts Erin kept teasing him about. He glanced over to admire how amazing she looked in her navy sundress emblazoned with tiny white stars.

Stung by a twinge of guilt, he asked, "Sure you wouldn't rather be at the Fourth of July festival in town?"

"I'm going for another kind of fireworks this year." Erin winked as she smoothed a red gingham tablecloth across Kent's old wooden picnic table.

Kent didn't see how he could possibly love this woman any more than he already did. Grinning, he laid down his tongs and stepped away from the grill. "Then why don't you come on over here and get the fireworks started?"

Avery, rolling in the grass with Skip, gave an annoyed groan. "Are you guys going to kiss again?"

"You betcha." Kent slipped an arm around Erin's waist to draw her close. As he lowered his lips to hers, her eyes darkened in a tender look that made his chest ache.

When the kiss ended, Erin sighed in a fake swoon. "I'm definitely seeing stars now!" Then she gasped. "Kent—the steaks!"

He whirled around to see flames leaping from the grill. Grabbing tongs and a platter, he whisked the meat to safety. "You did say you preferred your rib eye well-done."

"Do I have a choice?" Erin rolled her eyes. She sent Avery inside to wash her hands, then uncovered the side dishes she'd brought.

They sat down to eat in the shade of an oak tree, and as Kent offered grace, he stammered once or twice in amazement over how blessed he was. For the past month, he and Erin had spent every spare moment together, and as they shared more and more of their lives with each other, the scars of their pasts slowly faded. Erin was flourishing after signing the partnership agreement with Wanda, and they'd renamed the shop WE Design, combining the initials of their first names. In the meantime, Kent continued meeting with Pastor Terry, and Erin had joined them a few times for a better understanding of Kent's struggles since his military service.

A big milestone came when Erin received word from Lauren Hall that Payne had been found guilty. His medical license had been revoked, and he had been given a two-year suspended sentence. He'd also have to pay a hefty fine, attend AA meetings and anger management classes, and perform one year of community service.

Kent wasn't sure the penalty was stiff enough, but Erin seemed to have forgiven her ex-husband, and together they'd prayed for God to change the man's heart.

After the meal, as they enjoyed slices of watermelon for dessert, Kent's cell phone rang. He checked his watch—*right on cue*—and excused himself to take the call.

Returning to the table, he straddled the bench. "That was Christina. They're heading into town for the fireworks and wondered if Avery would like to go along."

Watermelon juice dripping off her chin, Avery bounced on the seat. "Can I, Mom?"

"I guess so—after you wash your face." As Avery rushed inside, Erin slanted a dubious look at Kent. "Interesting that Christina happened to call your phone and not mine."

"Yeah, funny, isn't it?" Kent busied himself finishing his melon.

Shortly, the Austin family arrived, and Avery climbed in beside Eva in the back seat of Seth's pickup. Through Seth's open window, Kent gave him a fist bump. "Perfect timing," he whispered. "Can't thank you enough."

"What are you two conspiring about?" Erin asked as she helped Avery get buckled in.

"They're just being guys," Christina said from the passenger seat. "Enjoy the rest of your evening. We'll bring Avery back here after the fireworks are over."

Watching Seth drive away, Kent suffered a major attack of nerves. He'd planned out every detail of this evening—well, except for the overdone steaks—but now he wondered if he was rushing things. Maybe in another month or two or five…

Erin linked her arm through his. "Want to tell me what's really going on here, cowboy?"

One look in her sparkling blue eyes and his doubts subsided. "Let's take a walk."

The leisurely stroll allowed him to collect his thoughts and slow his racing heart. With Skip ambling along beside them, they talked about inconsequential things while wandering beneath a sky rapidly filling with stars. When they neared the front porch, Kent invited Erin to sit beside him on the top step.

"It's so perfectly beautiful here." She tucked her hand into Kent's and gazed toward the heavens.

"Sure is," he said, looking only at her. He lifted her hand to his lips. "Erin…" His throat had gone dry, his voice rough with emotion. He waited until she turned to face him. "Erin, you know how much I love you."

She nodded, her eyes suddenly welling up. "I love you, too. More than I thought I could love anyone."

"You've changed me, Erin. Your courage, your faith in God—you inspire me. You make me feel alive and whole."

Releasing a soft laugh, she caressed his cheek. "From the day I wandered into your pasture and you gave me that wild ride on Jasmine, you've been changing me, too. You made me believe in myself. You made me believe in love again."

Hands shaking, Kent fumbled in his shirt pocket, drawing out a tiny packet of white tissue paper. He laid the packet in Erin's open palm and carefully unfolded it to reveal a delicate gold ring with a sapphire setting.

She gasped. "Kent, it's beautiful." Then her eyes filled with questions. "Is this…"

He slid the ring onto her finger. "It was my grandmother's engagement ring, and now it's yours, if you'll accept it. I realize there's still a lot we don't know about each other, but I figure we have a lifetime to learn. I want to marry you, Erin. I want to spend the rest of my life making you happy."

She threw her arms around his neck. "If I were any happier, I'd burst."

Sealing their promise with a kiss, Kent said a mental thank-you to all the friends and family whose support, encouragement and timely words of wisdom had brought him to this moment. But most of all, he thanked God for the day this red-haired, basket-weaving beauty had found her way into his life...and heart.

* * * * *

If you enjoyed this story, pick up these other books by Myra Johnson:

Rancher for the Holidays
Her Hill Country Cowboy
Hill Country Reunion

Available now from Love Inspired!

Find more great reads at
www.LoveInspired.com.

Dear Reader,

I hope you enjoyed this visit to the Texas Hill Country for Erin and Kent's love story. Writing about two characters dealing with painful pasts, I remember so well when I came upon this verse from Isaiah: *when thou passest through the waters, I will be with thee; and through the rivers, they shall not overflow thee…*

In this life, there will always be difficulties, yet God never abandons us. Even in the darkest times when God may feel so far away, we can trust Him to see us *through* to the other side.

If you or someone you know is living in an abusive situation, be assured that enduring in silence is *not* God's will. God desires that everyone should come to saving faith in Him, so holding the abuser accountable—always from a place of safety and involving the authorities when necessary—is an act of grace. The National Domestic Violence Hotline, www.thehotline.org/is-this-abuse/, offers resources and advice.

Thank you for being one of my faithful readers. You complete the journey from idea to fully realized story. I'd love to hear from you, so please contact me through my website, www.myrajohnson.com, or write to me c/o Love Inspired Books, Harlequin Enterprises, 233 Broadway, Suite 1001, New York, NY 10279.

With blessings and gratitude,
Myra

COMING NEXT MONTH FROM
Love Inspired®

Available May 21, 2019

HIS SUITABLE AMISH WIFE
Women of Lancaster County • by Rebecca Kertz

Helping widower Reuben Miller care for his baby was just supposed to be a favor for a friend. But when Ellie Stoltzfus falls for father and son, can she win Reuben's heart, despite his vow that he'll marry again only to give his child a mother—*not* for love?

HER OKLAHOMA RANCHER
Mercy Ranch • by Brenda Minton

Paralyzed veteran Eve Vincent is happy with the life she's built for herself at Mercy Ranch—until her ex-fiancé shows up with a baby. Their best friends died and named Eve and Ethan Forester as guardians. But can they put their differences aside and build a future together?

HIGH COUNTRY HOMECOMING
Rocky Mountain Ranch • by Roxanne Rustand

When he starts his life over after a medical discharge from the marines, the last thing Devlin Langford wants is for his childhood nemesis to rent a cabin on his ranch. But pretty Chloe Kenner and her sunny smile might be just what he needs to begin healing.

WINNING THE RANCHER'S HEART
Three Brothers Ranch • by Arlene James

Barrel racer Jeri Bogman arrives at Ryder Smith's ranch claiming she wants to buy property, but she has another plan entirely. A tragedy in her past is shrouded in secrets, and growing close to Ryder is the key to finding the truth.

THE TEXAN'S SECRET DAUGHTER
Cowboys of Diamondback Ranch • by Jolene Navarro

When Elijah De La Rosa runs into his ex-wife—the one person he hasn't apologized to for his youthful mistakes—he's shocked to discover they have a five-year-old daughter. But can he convince her he's a changed man worthy of the title *daddy*...and, possibly, *husband*?

THEIR BABY BLESSING
by Heidi McCahan

After leaving the navy, Gage Westbrook adopts a new mission—fulfilling his promise to look out for the baby boy his late friend never met. But when he loses his heart to the child and his stand-in mom, Skye Tomlinson, will Gage gain an instant family?

———————

LOOK FOR THESE AND OTHER LOVE INSPIRED BOOKS WHEREVER BOOKS ARE SOLD, INCLUDING MOST BOOKSTORES, SUPERMARKETS, DISCOUNT STORES AND DRUGSTORES.

LICNM0519

Get 4 FREE REWARDS!

We'll send you 2 FREE Books plus 2 FREE Mystery Gifts.

Love Inspired® books feature contemporary inspirational romances with Christian characters facing the challenges of life and love.

FREE
Value Over
$20

YES! Please send me 2 FREE Love Inspired® Romance novels and my 2 FREE mystery gifts (gifts are worth about $10 retail). After receiving them, if I don't wish to receive any more books, I can return the shipping statement marked "cancel." If I don't cancel, I will receive 6 brand-new novels every month and be billed just $5.24 for the regular-print edition or $5.74 each for the larger-print edition in the U.S., or $5.74 each for the regular-print edition or $6.24 each for the larger-print edition in Canada. That's a savings of at least 13% off the cover price. It's quite a bargain! Shipping and handling is just 50¢ per book in the U.S. and 75¢ per book in Canada.* I understand that accepting the 2 free books and gifts places me under no obligation to buy anything. I can always return a shipment and cancel at any time. The free books and gifts are mine to keep no matter what I decide.

Choose one: ☐ **Love Inspired® Romance Regular-Print** (105/305 IDN GMY4) ☐ **Love Inspired® Romance Larger-Print** (122/322 IDN GMY4)

Name (please print)

Address   Apt. #

City   State/Province   Zip/Postal Code

Mail to the **Reader Service:**
IN U.S.A.: P.O. Box 1341, Buffalo, NY 14240-8531
IN CANADA: P.O. Box 603, Fort Erie, Ontario L2A 5X3

Want to try 2 free books from another series? Call 1-800-873-8635 or visit www.ReaderService.com.

SPECIAL EXCERPT FROM

Laura Beth is determined to leave Cedar Grove to find love and start a family, but then an Englischer and his baby are stranded on her property. Could her greatest wish be right in front of her?

Read on for a sneak preview of
The Wish *by Patricia Davids*
available May 2019 from HQN Books!

"What is that?" Laura Beth Yoder wondered out loud.

She stepped out onto the porch and folded her arms tightly across her chest. She closed her eyes and turned her head slightly, waiting for a break in the sound of the storm. There it was again.

It was a car horn. She was sure of it. Was someone in trouble? Lifting a raincoat from the hook by the door, Laura Beth pulled it on and zipped it up to her chin. She walked out onto the end of the porch.

Was she really going out into this storm? Whenever the wind died a little, she heard the horn again. It sounded like it was coming from the bridge.

The sight that met her eyes when she reached the top of the lane sent her heart hammering in terror.

A car had plowed into the rocky embankment of the creek at the edge of the bridge. The floodwaters swirling under it would continue to rise. They were already at the bottom of the car doors.

A dark-haired man sat slumped over the steering wheel. Blood trickled from his temple.

"Mister, you need to get out!"

He slowly raised a hand to the side of his head and blinked. She pulled on the door handle. It was locked. "You have to get out."

A high-pitched wail came from inside. She shone her light in the back seat. A baby sat strapped into a car seat. Water was already seeping inside the vehicle. She yanked on the rear door handle, but it was locked, too. The car shifted again. How long before the floodwaters swept them away? Was she going to watch this innocent child die?

She pulled on the door with all her might. It wouldn't budge.

She'd never felt more alone and powerless. Fighting down her panic, she searched for a way to break the glass. She hurried to shore, found a large rock and returned to the car. Praying the glass wouldn't injure the child, she closed her eyes and slammed the stone against the window.

Don't miss
The Wish *by Patricia Davids,*
available May 2019 wherever
HQN Books and ebooks are sold.

www.Harlequin.com

Looking for inspiration in tales
of hope, faith and heartfelt romance?

Check out **Love Inspired**® and
Love Inspired® **Suspense** books!

New books available every month!

CONNECT WITH US AT:

Facebook.com/groups/HarlequinConnection

Facebook.com/HarlequinBooks

Twitter.com/HarlequinBooks

Instagram.com/HarlequinBooks

Pinterest.com/HarlequinBooks

ReaderService.com

Inspirational Romance to Warm Your Heart and Soul

Join our social communities to connect with other readers who share your love!

Sign up for the Love Inspired newsletter at **www.LoveInspired.com** to be the first to find out about upcoming titles, special promotions and exclusive content.

CONNECT WITH US AT:

Facebook.com/groups/HarlequinConnection

 Facebook.com/LoveInspiredBooks

 Twitter.com/LoveInspiredBks

LISOCIAL2018